NS

'A compassionate, witty and unforgettable masterpiece'
Daily Telegraph

'At once nostalgic and satiric, a resplendent fable and sombre parable, *Of Love and Other Demons* is a further marvellous manifestation of the enchantment and the disenchantment that his native Colombia always stirs in Márquez' *Sunday Times*

'Márquez tells a story of forbidden love, but he demonstrates once again the vigour of his own passion: the daring and irresistible coupling oh history and imagination' *Time*

'As enchanting as anything Márquez has ever written' *Observer*

'Márquez writes in this lyrical, magical language that no-one else can do' Salman Rushdie

'Of all the living authors known to me, only one is undoubtedly touched by genius: Gabriel García Márquez' *Sunday Telegraph*

'Tragi-comic, acerbic, supernatural and mysterious. Pleasurable on many levels. Superb and intensely readable' *Time Out*

'The most important writer of fiction in any language'
Bill Clinton

'Brilliantly moving' *New York Times Book Review*

'One of this century's most evocative writers' Anne Tyler

ABOUT THE AUTHOR

Gabriel García Márquez was born in 1927 in Aracataca, Colombia. His most recent book, *Memories of My Melancholy Whores* (2005), is his first new novel to be published in a decade and is now available in paperback from Penguin. He is the author of several novels, works of non-fiction and collections of short stories, including *Leaf Storm* (1955); *One Hundred Years of Solitude* (1967); *The Autumn of the Patriarch* (1975); *Chronicle of a Death Foretold* (1981) and *The General in His Labyrinth* (1989). He was awarded the Nobel Prize for Literature in 1982.

Of Love and Other Demons

GABRIEL GARCÍA MÁRQUEZ

TRANSLATED FROM THE SPANISH
BY EDITH GROSSMAN

PENGUIN BOOKS

PENGUIN BOOKS

Published by the Penguin Group
Penguin Books Ltd, 80 Strand, London WC2R ORL, England
Penguin Group (USA) Inc., 375 Hudson Street, New York, New York 10014, USA
Penguin Group (Canada), 90 Eglinton Avenue East, Suite 700, Toronto, Ontario, Canada M4P 2Y3
(a division of Pearson Penguin Canada Inc.)
Penguin Ireland, 25 St Stephen's Green, Dublin 2, Ireland (a division of Penguin Books Ltd)
Penguin Group (Australia), 250 Camberwell Road, Camberwell, Victoria 3124, Australia
(a division of Pearson Australia Group Pty Ltd)
Penguin Books India Pvt Ltd, 11 Community Centre, Panchsheel Park, New Delhi – 110 017, India
Penguin Group (NZ), 67 Apollo Drive, Rosedale, North Shore 0632, New Zealand
(a division of Pearson New Zealand Ltd)
Penguin Books (South Africa) (Pty) Ltd, 24 Sturdee Avenue,
Rosebank, Johannesburg 2196, South Africa

Penguin Books Ltd, Registered Offices: 80 Strand, London WC2R ORL, England

www.penguin.com

First published in Spain as *Del amor y otros demonios* by Mondadori 1994
This translation first published in Great Britain by Jonathan Cape 1995
First published in Penguin Books 1996
This edition published 2008
001

Printed in England by Clays Ltd, St Ives plc

ISBN: 978-0-241-98039-2

www.greenpenguin.co.uk

For Carmen Balcells
bathed in tears

For the hair, it seems, is less concerned in the resurrection than other parts of the body.

THOMAS AQUINAS
On the Integrity of Resurrected Bodies,
Question 80, Chapter 5

October 26, 1949, was not a day filled with important news. Maestro Clemente Manuel Zabala, editor-in-chief of the newspaper where I learned the essentials of being a reporter, concluded our morning meeting with two or three routine suggestions. He did not assign a specific story to any writer. A few minutes later he was informed by telephone that the burial crypts of the old Convent of Santa Clara were being emptied, and with few illusions he said to me, 'Stop by there and see if you can come up with anything.'

The historic convent of the Clarissan nuns, which had been turned into a hospital a century earlier, was to be sold, and a five-star hotel built in its place. The gradual collapse of the roof had left its beautiful chapel exposed to the elements, but three generations of bishops and abbesses and other eminent personages were still buried there. The first step was to empty the crypts, transfer the remains to anyone who claimed them and bury the rest in a common grave.

I was surprised by the crudeness of the procedure. Laborers opened the tombs with pickaxes and hoes, took out the rotting coffins, which broke apart with the simple act of moving them, and separated bones from the jumble of dust, shreds of clothing and desiccated hair. The more illustrious the dead . . . the more arduous the labor, because the workers had to rummage through the remains and sift the debris with great care in order to retrieve precious stones and articles of gold and silver.

The foreman copied the information that was on each stone into a notebook, arranged the bones into distinct piles and placed a sheet of paper with a name on top of every mound to keep them all separate. And so the first thing I saw when I entered the temple was a long line of stacked bones, heated by the savage October sun pouring in through the holes in the roof and with no more identity than a name scrawled in pencil on a piece of paper. Almost half a century later I can still feel the confusion produced in me by that terrible testimony to the devastating passage of the years.

There, among many others, were a viceroy of Peru and his secret lover; Don Toribio de Cáceres y Virtudes, bishop of this diocese; several of the convent's abbesses, including Mother Josefa Miranda; and the bachelor of arts Don Cristóbal de Eraso, who devoted half his life to building the coffered ceilings. One crypt was sealed with the stone of the second Marquis de Casalduero, Don Ygnacio de Alfaro y Dueñas, but when it was opened they found it empty; it had never been used. The remains of his marquise, however, Doña Olalla de Mendoza, had their own stone in the adjacent crypt. The foreman attached no importance to this: it was not unusual for an American-born aristocrat to have prepared his own tomb and be buried in another.

The surprise lay in the third niche of the high altar, on the side where the Gospels were kept. The stone shattered at the first blow of the pickax and a stream of living hair the intense color of copper spilled out of the crypt. The foreman, with the help of the laborers, attempted to uncover all the hair, and the more of it they brought out, the longer and more abundant it seemed, until at last the final strands appeared still attached to the skull of a young girl. Nothing else remained in the niche except a few small scattered bones, and on the dressed stone eaten away by saltpeter only a given name with no surnames was legible: SIERVA MARÍA DE TODOS LOS ÁNGELES. *Spread out on the floor, the splendid hair measured twenty-two meters, eleven centimeters.*

The impassive foreman explained that human hair grew a centimeter a month after death, and twenty-two meters seemed a good average for two hundred years. I, on the other hand, did not think it so trivial a matter, for when I was a boy my grandmother had told me the legend of a little twelve-year-old marquise with hair that trailed behind her like a bridal train, who had died of rabies caused by a dog bite and was venerated in the towns along the Caribbean coast for the many miracles she had performed. The idea that the tomb might be hers was my news item for the day, and the origin of this book.

GABRIEL GARCÍA MÁRQUEZ
Cartagena de Indias, 1994

One

An ash-gray dog with a white blaze on its forehead burst onto the rough terrain of the market on the first Sunday in December, knocked down tables of fried food, overturned Indians' stalls and lottery kiosks and bit four people who happened to cross its path. Three of them were black slaves. The fourth, Sierva María de Todos los Ángeles, the only child of the Marquis de Casalduero, had come there with a mulatta servant to buy a string of bells for the celebration of her twelfth birthday.

They had been instructed not to go beyond the Arcade of the Merchants, but the maid ventured as far as the drawbridge in the slum of Getsemaní, attracted by the crowd at the slavers' port, where a shipment of blacks from Guinea was being sold at a discount. For the past week a ship belonging to the Compañia Gaditana de Negros had been awaited with dismay because of an unexplainable series of deaths on board. In an attempt at concealment, the unweighted corpses were thrown into the water. The tide brought them to the surface and washed the bodies, disfigured by swelling and a strange magenta coloring, up on the beach. The vessel lay anchored outside the bay, for everyone feared an outbreak of some African plague, until it was verified that the cause of death was food poisoning.

At the time the dog ran through the market the surviving cargo had already been sold at reduced prices on account of poor health, and the owners were attempting to compensate for the loss with a single article worth all the rest: an Abyssinian female almost two meters tall, who was smeared with cane molasses instead of the usual commercial oil, and whose beauty was so unsettling it seemed untrue. She had a slender nose, a rounded skull, slanted eyes, all her teeth and the equivocal bearing of a Roman gladiator. She had not been branded in the slave pen, and they did not call out her age and the state of her health. Instead, she was put on sale for the simple fact of her beauty. The price the Governor paid, without bargaining and in cash, was her weight in gold.

It was a common occurrence for a stray dog to bite people as it chased after cats or fought turkey buzzards for the carrion in the streets, and it was even more common during the times of prosperity and crowds when the Galleon Fleet stopped on its way to the Portobelo Fair. No one lost sleep over four or five dog bites in a single day, least of all over an almost invisible wound like the one on Sierva María's left ankle. And therefore the maid was not alarmed. She treated the bite herself with lemon and sulfur and washed the bloodstain from the girl's petticoats, and no one gave a thought to anything but the festivities for her twelfth birthday.

Earlier that morning, Bernarda Cabrera, the girl's mother and the untitled spouse of the Marquis de Casalduero, had taken a dramatic purge: seven grains of antimony in a glass of sugared rosewater. She had been an untamed mestiza of the so-called shopkeeper aristocracy: seductive, rapacious, brazen, with a hunger in her womb that could have satisfied an entire barracks. In a few short years, however, she had been erased from the world by her abuse of fermented honey and cacao tablets. Her

Gypsy eyes were extinguished and her wits dulled, she shat blood and vomited bile, her siren's body became as bloated and coppery as a three-day-old corpse and she broke wind in pestilential explosions that startled the mastiffs. She almost never left her bedroom, and when she did she was nude or wearing a silk tunic with nothing underneath, which made her seem more naked than if she wore nothing at all.

She had already moved her bowels seven times when the maid who had accompanied Sierva María returned but told her nothing about the dog bite. She did, however, comment on the scandal at the port caused by the sale of the slave woman. 'If she's as beautiful as you claim, she might be Abyssinian,' said Bernarda. But even if she were the Queen of Sheba, it did not seem possible that anyone would pay her weight in gold.

'They must have meant in weighed gold pesos,' she said.

'No, as much gold as the black woman weighs,' the maid explained.

'A slave two meters tall weighs at least 120 pounds,' said Bernarda. 'And no woman, white or black, is worth 120 pounds of gold, unless she shits diamonds.'

No one had been more astute than Bernarda in the slave trade, and she knew that if the Governor had bought the Abyssinian it could not be for something as sublime as serving in his kitchen. Just then she heard the first hornpipes and firecrackers of a fiesta, followed by the furious barking of the mastiffs in their cages. She went out to the orange grove to see what it could be.

Don Ygnacio de Alfaro y Dueñas, the second Marquis de Casalduero and Lord of Darien, had also heard the music, from his siesta hammock hanging between two orange trees in the grove. He was a funereal, effeminate man, as pale as a lily because the bats drained his blood while he slept. He wore a Bedouin djellaba in the house, and a Toledan biretta that increased his forlorn appearance. When he saw his wife as naked as the day God brought her into the world, he anticipated her question and asked, 'What music is that?'

'I don't know,' she said. 'What's the date?'

The Marquis did not know. He really must have felt quite puzzled to ask his wife anything, and she must have felt complete relief from her bilious attack to reply with no sarcasm. He had sat up in the hammock, intrigued, when the firecrackers exploded again.

'Good Lord!' he exclaimed. 'Can it be that date already?'

The house adjoined the Divina Pastora Asylum for Female Lunatics. Agitated by the music and fireworks, the patients had appeared on the terrace that overlooked the orange grove, and they celebrated each explosion with ovations. The Marquis called up to them, asking where the fiesta was, and they cleared away his doubts. It was December seventh, the Feast of Saint Ambrose the Bishop, and the music and fireworks thundering in the slaves' courtyard were in honor of Sierva María. The Marquis slapped his forehead.

'Of course,' he said. 'How old is she?'

'Twelve,' replied Bernarda.

'Only twelve?' he said, lying down again in the hammock. 'How slow life is!'

The house had been the pride of the city until the beginning of the century. Now it was a melancholy ruin, and the large empty spaces and the many objects out of place made it seem as if the occupants were in the process of moving. The drawing rooms had kept their checkerboard marble floors and teardrop chandeliers draped in cobwebs. The rooms still in use were cool in any weather because of their thick masonry walls and many years of enclosure, and even more because of the December breezes that came whistling through the cracks. Everything was saturated with the oppressive damp of neglect and gloom. All that remained of the seignorial dignities of the first Marquis were the five hunting mastiffs that guarded the nights.

The resounding courtyard of the slaves, where Sierva María's birthday was being celebrated, had been another city within the city in the time of the first Marquis. This continued under his heir for as long as the illicit traffic in slaves and flour, directed in secret by Bernarda from the Mahates sugar plantation, had lasted. Now all that splendor was a thing of the past. Bernarda had been extinguished by her insatiable vices, and the slave-yard reduced to two wooden shacks with roofs of bitter palm, where the last scraps of greatness had already been consumed.

Dominga de Adviento, a formidable black woman who ruled the house with an iron fist until the night before her death, was the link between these two worlds. Tall and bony, and possessed of an almost clairvoyant intelligence, it was she who had reared Sierva María. Dominga de Adviento became a Catholic without renouncing her Yoruban beliefs, and she practiced both religions at the same time, and at random. Her soul was healthy and at peace, she said, because what she did not find in one faith was there in the other. She was also the only human being with the authority to mediate between the Marquis and his wife, and they both accommodated her. Only she could drive the slaves out with a broom when she discovered them in the vacant rooms committing calamitous acts of sodomy or fornicating with bartered women. But after she died they would flee the shacks to escape the midday heat and stretch out on the floor in every corner, or scrape the crust out of the rice pots and eat it, or play with the *macuco* and the *tarabilla* in the cool corridors. In that oppressive world where no one was free, Sierva María was: she alone, and there alone. And so that was where her birthday was celebrated, in her true home and with her true family.

In the midst of so much music it was difficult to imagine dancing more silent than that of the Marquis's slaves and a few blacks from other distinguished households, who brought whatever they could. The girl displayed just who she was. She could dance with more grace and fire than the Africans, sing in voices different from her own in the various languages of Africa, agitate the birds and animals when she imitated their voices. By order of Dominga de Adviento, the younger slave girls would blacken her face with soot. They hung Santería necklaces over her baptism scapular and looked after her hair, which had never been cut and would have interfered with her walking if they had not braided it into loops every day.

She had begun to blossom under a combination of contradictory influences. She inherited very little from her mother. She had her father's thin body, however, and his irremediable shyness, pale skin, eyes of taciturn blue and the pure copper of her radiant hair. Her movements were so stealthy that she seemed an invisible creature. Frightened by her strange nature, her mother had hung a cowbell around the girl's wrist so she would not lose track of her in the shadows of the house.

Two days after the fiesta the maid mentioned in passing to Bernarda that a dog had bitten Sierva María. Bernarda thought about it as she took her sixth hot bath of the day with perfumed soaps before going to bed, and by the time she returned to her room she had forgotten it. She did not remember it again until the following night, when the mastiffs barked until dawn for no reason, and she was afraid they had rabies. Then she took a candlestick to the shacks in the courtyard and found Sierva María asleep in the hammock of Indian royal palm she had inherited from Dominga de Adviento. Since the maid had not told her where the bite was located, Bernarda raised the girl's chemise and examined her inch by inch, using the light to follow the penitential braid that curled around her body like a lion's tail. At last she found it: a little break in the skin on her left ankle, with a scab of dried blood and some almost invisible abrasions on the heel.

Cases of rabies were neither limited nor insignificant in the history of the city. The most notorious was that of a street peddler who plied his trade with a trained monkey whose actions were almost indistinguishable from those of humans. The animal contracted rabies during the naval siege by the English, bit its owner on the face and escaped to the nearby hills. The unfortunate man was clubbed to death while suffering fearful hallucinations, which mothers still sang about many years later in popular ballads meant to frighten children. Before two weeks had passed a horde of satanic macaque monkeys descended from the hills in the full light of day. They devastated pigsties and henhouses and then, howling and choking on their own frothing blood, burst into the cathedral during a Te Deum celebrating the defeat of the English fleet. Yet the most terrible dramas did not pass into the annals of history, for they occurred among the population of blacks, who spirited away the victims to cure them by African magic in the settlements of runaway slaves.

Despite so many dreadful portents, no one – white, black, or Indian – even gave a thought to rabies or any other disease that was slow to incubate until the first irreparable symptoms made their appearance. Bernarda Cabrera proceeded according to the same criterion. She thought that the gossip of slaves traveled faster and farther than the inventions of Christians and that even a simple dog bite might damage the family's honor. She was so certain of her reasoning that she did not mention the matter to her husband or think about it again until the following Sunday, when the maid went to the market alone and saw the carcass of a dog that had been hung from an almond tree to let everyone know it had died of rabies. One glance was all she needed to recognize the blaze on the forehead and the ash-gray coat of the dog that had bitten Sierva María. But Bernarda was not concerned when she heard the news. There was no reason to be: the wound was dry and not even a trace of the abrasions remained.

December had begun with foul weather but soon recovered its amethyst afternoons and nights of antic breezes. Christmas was more joyous than in other years because of the good news from Spain. But the city was not what it had once been. The principal slave market had been moved to Havana, and the miners and ranchers in these kingdoms of Terra Firma preferred to buy contraband labor at lower prices in the English Antilles. And so there were two cities: one busy and crowded for the six months the galleons remained in port, and the other that drowsed for the rest of the year as it waited for them to return.

Nothing more was known about those who had been bitten until the beginning of January, when a vagabond Indian woman called Sagunta knocked on the Marquis's door at the sacred hour of siesta. She was very old and she walked barefoot in the full sun, leaning on a staff of *carreto* wood and wrapped from head to toe in a white sheet. She was notorious for being a mender of maidenheads and an abortionist, although this was balanced by her admirable reputation for knowing Indian secrets that could heal the incurable.

The Marquis stood in the entranceway and received her with great reluctance, and it took him some time to understand what she wanted, for she was a woman who favored slow and intricate circumlocutions. She made so many twists and turns in order to say anything that the Marquis lost patience.

'Whatever it is, just tell me with no more Latinizing,' he said.

'We are threatened by a plague of rabies,' said Sagunta, 'and I am the only one who has the keys of Saint Hubert, protector of hunters and healer of the rabid.'

'I see no reason for a plague,' said the Marquis. 'As far as I know, no comets or eclipses have been forecast, and our sins are not great enough for God to be concerned with us.'

Sagunta informed him that there would be a total eclipse of the sun in March and gave him a complete account of all those bitten on the first Sunday in December. Two had disappeared, no doubt spirited away by their people to try to cure them with magic, and a third had died of rabies by the second week. A fourth victim, not bitten but only spattered by the dog's spittle, lay dying in the Amor de Dios Hospital. The chief constable had ordered a hundred stray dogs poisoned so far this month. In another week not one would be left alive on the streets.

'Be that as it may, I do not know what any of this has to do with me,' said the Marquis. 'Least of all at so irregular an hour.'

'Your daughter was the first to be bitten,' said Sagunta.

The Marquis responded with great conviction, 'If that were true, I would have been the first to know.'

He believed the girl was well, and it did not seem possible that something so serious could have happened to her without his knowledge. And therefore he considered the visit concluded and went back to finish his siesta.

That afternoon, however, he looked for Sierva María in the servants' courtyards. She was helping to skin rabbits, and her face was painted black, her feet were bare and her head was wrapped in the red turban used by slave women. He asked her if she had been bitten by a dog, and the answer was a categorical no. But that night Bernarda confirmed it was true. The Marquis was bewildered and asked, 'Then why does Sierva deny it?'

'Because she wouldn't tell the truth even by mistake,' said Bernarda.

'Then it is necessary to take action,' said the Marquis, 'because the dog had rabies.'

'No,' said Bernarda, 'the dog must have died because it bit her. This happened in December, and the little hussy is like a rose.'

They both continued to be mindful of the growing rumors regarding the seriousness of the plague and against their own wishes were forced to speak again about questions of common interest as they had in the days when they hated each other less. For him the matter was clear. He always believed he loved his daughter, but the fear of rabies obliged the Marquis to admit to himself that this was a lie for the sake of convenience. Bernarda, on the other hand, did not even ask herself the question, for she knew very well she did not love the girl and the girl did not love her, and both things seemed fitting. A good part of the hatred each of them felt for Sierva María was caused by the other's qualities in her. Nevertheless, to preserve her honor, Bernarda was prepared to play out the farce of shedding tears and mourning like a grief-stricken mother, on the condition that the girl's death have a seemly cause.

'It doesn't matter what,' she specified, 'as long as it's not a dog's disease.'

At that moment, as if in a blinding flash from heaven, the Marquis understood the meaning of his life.

'The girl is not going to die,' he said with determination. 'But if she must die, it shall be of whatever God wills.'

On Tuesday he went to the Amor de Dios Hospital, on

San Lázaro Hill, to see the rabies victim Sagunta had mentioned to him. He was not aware that his carriage, with its mortuary crepe, would be viewed as yet another symptom of incubating disaster, because for many years he had not left his house except on great occasions, and for many more years there had been no occasions greater than calamitous ones.

The city lay submerged in its centuries-long torpor, but there was no lack of observers to glimpse the gaunt face and elusive eyes of the tentative nobleman in mourning taffetas as his carriage left the walled district and drove through the countryside to San Lázaro Hill. At the hospital, the lepers lying on the brick floors saw him walk in with his dead man's gait, and they barred his way to beg for alms. In the pavilion that housed raving lunatics he found the rabies victim tied to a pillar.

He was an old mulatto with a beard and hair like cotton. By now half his body was paralyzed, but the disease had endowed the other half with so much strength that he had to be tied to keep him from smashing himself to pieces against the walls. His story left no doubt: he had been attacked by the same ash-colored dog with the white blaze that had bitten Sierva María. In fact, only the animal's spittle had touched him, but that was on a chronic ulcer on his calf, not healthy skin. This detail was not enough to reassure the Marquis, who left the hospital horrified by the sight of the dying man and with no glimmer of hope for Sierva María.

As he was returning to the city along the cornice of the hill, he saw a man of imposing appearance sitting on a stone in the road next to a dead horse. The Marquis told the driver to stop, and only when the man stood did he recognize the licenciate Abrenuncio de Sa Pereira Cao, the most notable and controversial physician in the city. Identical to the King of Clubs, he wore a broad-brimmed hat for the sun, riding boots and the black cloak favored by educated libertines. His greeting to the Marquis was not at all usual.

'*Benedictus qui venit in nomine veritatis*,' he said.

His horse had not survived the descent of the same slope it had ascended at a trot, and its heart had burst. Neptuno, the Marquis's coachman, attempted to remove the saddle from the animal. The owner stopped him.

'What use do I have for a saddle if I have no one to saddle,' he said. 'Leave it to rot along with him.'

The coachman had to help the doctor into the carriage because of his puerile corpulence, and the Marquis paid him the honor of having him sit on his right. Abrenuncio was thinking about his horse.

'It is as if I had lost half my body,' he sighed.

'Nothing is easier to resolve than the death of a horse,' said the Marquis.

Abrenuncio became more animated. 'This one was different,' he said. 'If I had the means, I would have him buried in holy ground.' He looked at the Marquis to see his reaction, and concluded, 'He turned 100 in October.'

'No horse lives that long,' said the Marquis.

'I can prove it,' said the doctor.

On Tuesdays he offered his services at the Amor de Dios Hospital, treating the lepers who suffered from other diseases. He had been an outstanding student of the physician Juan Méndez Nieto, another Portuguese Jew who had emigrated to the Caribbean because of the persecution in Spain, and had inherited his evil reputation for necromancy and a loose tongue; but no one cast doubt on his learning. His disputes with other physicians, who would not forgive his incredible successes or uncommon methods, were constant and bloody. He had invented a pill to be taken once a year, which enhanced one's health and lengthened one's life but caused such mental derangement for the first three days that no one but the doctor had dared to swallow it. At one time he had been in the habit of playing the harp at the bedside of his patients in order to sedate them with certain music composed for the purpose. He did not practice surgery, which he always considered an inferior art fit only for charlatans and barbers, and his terrifying specialty was predicting the day and hour his patients would die. Both his good name and his bad, however, were based on the same circumstance: it was said, and no one ever disproved it, that he had resurrected a dead man.

Despite his long experience, Abrenuncio felt pity for the rabies victim. 'The human body is not made to endure all the years that one may live,' he said. The Marquis did not miss a word of his exhaustive and colorful discourse, and spoke only when the doctor had nothing more to say.

'What can be done for that poor man?' he asked.

'Kill him,' said Abrenuncio.

The Marquis looked at him, appalled.

'At least that is what we would do if we were good Christians,' the impassive doctor continued. 'And never fear, Señor: there are more good Christians than one supposes.'

He was, in reality, referring to the poor Christians of every color, in the slums and in the countryside, who had the courage to poison the food of their rabid kin in order to spare them a ghastly death. At the end of the previous century an entire family had consumed poisoned soup because none of them had the heart to poison only a five-year-old boy.

'People believe that we physicians do not know that such things occur,' Abrenuncio concluded. 'That is not true, but we lack the moral authority to endorse them. What we do instead is what you have just seen. We commend the dying to Saint Hubert and tie them to a pillar in order to prolong and intensify their suffering.'

'Is there no other recourse?' asked the Marquis.

'After the initial outbreak of rabies, none at all,' said the doctor. He mentioned frivolous treatises that considered it a curable disease responsive to various prescriptions: liverwort, cinnabar, musk, silver mercury, *anagallis flore purpureo*. 'All rubbish,' he said. 'The fact is that some people contract rabies and others do not, and it is easy to say that if they did not, it was because of the medicines.' He looked into the eyes of the Marquis to be certain he was still awake, and concluded, 'Why are you so interested?'

'Out of pity,' the Marquis lied.

Through the window he contemplated the sea grown drowsy in the ennui of four o'clock and realized with a heavy heart that the swallows had returned. There was still no breeze. A group of children threw stones at a pelican gone astray on a muddy beach, and the Marquis followed the bird in its fugitive flight until it vanished among the brilliant domes of the fortified city.

The carriage entered the walled precincts at the inland Media Luna gate, and Abrenuncio guided the coachman through the bustling district of the artisans to his house. It was no easy task. Neptuno was more than seventy years old, and indecisive and shortsighted as well, and he was accustomed to having the horse move on its own through streets it knew better than he did. When at last they reached the house, Abrenuncio said goodbye at the door with a sentence from Horace.

'I am afraid I do not know Latin,' the Marquis apologized. 'There is no reason you should!' said Abrenuncio. And he said it in Latin of course.

The Marquis was so impressed that his first act when he returned home was the most unusual of his life. He ordered Neptuno to collect the dead horse on San Lázaro Hill and bury it in holy ground, and early the next day to send Abrenuncio the best horse in his stable.

After the ephemeral relief of antimony purges, Bernarda took as many as three consolatory enemas a day to extinguish the blaze in her belly or sank into as many as six hot baths with perfumed soaps to soothe her nerves. By this time there was nothing left of the person she had been when she married, a woman who devised commercial ventures and put them into effect with the assurance of a soothsayer, so great was her success, until the ill-fated afternoon she met Judas Iscariote and was swept away by misfortune.

She saw him for the first time inside a bullfighting corral erected at a fair, wrangling a fierce bull with his bare hands, almost naked, and unprotected. He was so handsome and bold she could not forget him. Days later she saw him again, dancing the *cumbé* at a carnival that she attended wearing a mask and disguised as a beggar and surrounded by her slave women dressed as marquises with necklaces and bracelets and earrings of gold and precious stones. Judas was in the center of a circle of onlookers, dancing with any woman who would pay him, and the authorities had to impose order to control the frantic yearning of his claimants. Bernarda asked him how much he cost. Judas replied as he danced: 'Half a *real*.'

Bernarda took off her mask.

'What I'm asking is how much you cost for the rest of your life,' she said.

Judas saw that with her mask removed she was not the beggar she had seemed. He let go of his partner and walked toward Bernarda with all the airs of a cabin boy to tell her his price.

'Five hundred gold pesos,' he said.

She measured him with the eye of a wary appraiser. He was enormous, with seal-colored skin, a rippling torso, narrow hips, graceful legs and beautiful hands that belied his position in life. Bernarda estimated, 'You're two meters tall.'

'And three centimeters,' he said.

Bernarda had him lower his head so that she could examine his teeth and she found the ammoniac breath of his armpits unsettling. He had all his teeth, and they were healthy and straight.

'Your master must be crazy if he thinks anyone's going to buy you for the price of a horse,' said Bernarda.

'I'm a free man and I'm selling myself,' he replied. And ended with a certain tone: 'Señora.'

'Marquise,' she said.

He made a courtier's bow that left her breathless, and

she bought him for half of what he had aspired to. 'Just for the pleasure of seeing him,' as she said. In return she respected both his condition as a free man and the time he spent wrangling his circus bull. She moved him into a room near her own, which had once belonged to the head groom, and from the first night, naked and with her door unbolted, she waited for him, confident he would come without being invited. But she had to wait two weeks, and did not sleep in peace because of the fire in her body.

The truth was that as soon as he learned who she was and saw the interior of the house, he re-established his slave's reserve. But when Bernarda had stopped waiting for him and slept in a nightgown and bolted the door, he came in through the window. The air in her room, rarefied by the ammoniac odor of his sweat, woke her. She heard the heavy breathing of a minotaur searching for her in the darkness, she felt the sultry heat of his body on top of her, his hands of prey grasping the neck of her nightgown and ripping it down the middle while his husky voice intoned in her ear, 'Whore, whore.' From that night on, Bernarda knew there was nothing else she wanted to do for the rest of her life.

She was mad about him. At night they would go to the dances in the slum districts, he dressed as a gentleman in a frock coat and round hat, which Bernarda bought to please him, and she in a variety of disguises at first, and then with her face unmasked. She showered him with the gold of chains, rings and bracelets and studded his teeth with diamonds. She thought she would die when she learned he took every woman who crossed his path to bed but in the end she settled for whatever was left over. It was during this time that Dominga de Adviento walked into Bernarda's bedroom at siesta, thinking she was at the sugar plantation, and found the two of them naked, making love on the floor. The slave woman stood with her hand on the latch, more confused than surprised.

'Don't just stand there like a corpse,' Bernarda shouted. 'Either get out or get down here with us.'

Dominga de Adviento left with a slam of the door that sounded to Bernarda like a slap in the face. That night she summoned her and threatened the most atrocious punishments if she said anything about what she had seen. 'Don't worry, white lady,' said the slave. 'You can forbid whatever you like, and I'll obey.' And she concluded, 'The trouble is you can't forbid what I think.'

If the Marquis did know anything, he was very good at pretending not to. After all, Sierva María was the only thing he still had in common with his wife, and he thought of Sierva María not as his daughter but as hers alone. And Bernarda did not think of the girl at all. She had put her so far out of her mind that when she returned from one of her extended stays at the sugar plantation, Bernarda mistook her for someone else because she had grown and changed so much. She called for her, examined her, questioned her about her life, but could not get her to say a single word.

'You're just like your father,' she said. 'A freak.'

Their attitudes had not changed on the day the Marquis returned from the Amor de Dios Hospital and announced to Bernarda his resolve to take up the reins of the household with a warlike hand. There was something frenetic in his urgency that left Bernarda speechless.

His first action was to return to the girl the bedroom that had belonged to her grandmother the Marquise, and that had been hers until Bernarda sent her to sleep with the slaves. Beneath the dust its former splendor remained intact: the imperial bed that the servants thought was gold because of the brilliance of its copper; the mosquito netting made of bridal tulle, the rich hangings of passementerie, the alabaster washstand and numerous bottles of perfumes and cosmetics lined in martial order on the dressing table; the portable chamber pot, the porcelain spittoon and vomitory, the entire illusory world that the old woman crippled by rheumatism had dreamed for the daughter she never had and the granddaughter she never saw.

While the slave women resurrected the bedroom, the Marquis went about imposing his will on the house. He drove away the slaves dozing in the shade of the arcades, and threatened beatings and slaves' prison for any who ever again relieved themselves in the corners or gambled in the rooms that had been closed off. These were not new decrees. They had been followed with far greater rigor when Bernarda gave the orders and Dominga de Adviento carried them out, and the Marquis took public delight in his historic declaration: 'In my house I do not say, I obey.' But when Bernarda succumbed to the quicksands of cacao, and Dominga de Adviento died, the slaves slipped back into the house with great stealth, first the women with their children to help in small tasks, and then the men without work, searching out the coolness of the corridors. Terrified by the specter of ruin, Bernarda ordered them to earn their keep by begging in the streets. In one of her crises she decided to free them all except for two or three house servants, but the Marquis opposed the idea with an illogical argument: 'If they are going to die of hunger, it is better for them to die here and not among strangers.'

He did not adhere to these easy formulas when Sierva María was bitten by the dog. He granted certain powers to the slave who seemed to have the greatest authority and be the most trustworthy and gave him instructions so harsh they shocked even Bernarda. Just after dark, when the house was in order for the first time since the death of Dominga de Adviento, he found Sierva María in the slave shack along with half a dozen young black women who were sleeping in hammocks criss-crossed at different levels. He woke them all to announce the rules of the new regime.

'From this day forward the girl lives in the house,' he said. 'And let it be known here and throughout the kingdom: she has only one family, and that family is white.'

The girl resisted when he tried to carry her in his arms to the bedroom, and he had to make her understand that a masculine order governed the world. Once they were in her grandmother's room, he replaced her slave's burlap chemise with a nightdress but could not make her say a word. Bernarda watched them from the door: the Marquis sitting on the bed and struggling with the buttons on the nightgown, which would not pass through the new buttonholes, and the girl standing in front of him and regarding him with an impassive expression. Bernarda could not restrain herself.

'Why don't you two get married?' she mocked. And since the Marquis ignored her, she added, 'Not a bad little business: You could breed American-born marquises with chicken feet and sell them to the circus.'

Something had changed in her as well. Despite the ferocity of her laughter, her face seemed less bitter, and at the bottom of her faithlessness lay a sediment of compassion that the Marquis did not see. As soon as he heard her leave, he said to the girl, 'She is a sow.'

He thought he detected a spark of interest. 'Do you know what a sow is?' he asked, eager for a reply. Sierva María did not grant him one. She allowed herself to be laid down on the bed, she allowed her head to be settled on the feather pillows, she allowed herself to be covered to the knees by the fine linen sheet fragrant with the scent of the cedar chest, and she did not bestow upon him the charity of a single glance. He felt a tremor of conscience. 'Do you pray before you sleep?'

The girl did not even look at him. Accustomed to a hammock, she curled into the fetal position and fell asleep without saying good night. The Marquis closed the mosquito netting with the greatest care so that the bats would not drain her blood as she slept. It was almost ten, and the chorus of madwomen was intolerable in the house redeemed by the expulsion of the slaves.

The Marquis set loose the mastiffs, and they raced to the grandmother's bedroom and sniffed at the cracks in the doors, panting and yelping. The Marquis scratched their heads with his fingertips and calmed them with the good news: 'It is Sierva, she will be living with us from now on.'

His sleep was brief and restless because the madwomen sang until two. The first thing he did when he woke with the roosters was to go to the girl's room, but she was not there. He found her in the shack with the slave women. The one sleeping closest to her woke with a start.

'She came by herself, Señor,' she said before he could ask the question. 'I didn't even know.'

The Marquis knew it was true. He asked which of them had been with Sierva María when the dog bit her. The only mulatta, whose name was Caridad del Cobre, identified herself, trembling with fear. The Marquis reassured her.

'Take charge of her as if you were Dominga de Adviento,' he said.

He explained her duties. He warned her not to let the girl out of her sight for an instant and to treat her with affection and understanding but not to pamper her. Most important of all, she was not to cross the thornbush fence he would place between the slave-yard and the rest of the house. In the morning when she awoke and at night before she went to sleep she was to give him a full report without his having to ask for it.

'Be careful what you do and how you do it,' he concluded. 'You will be the only one responsible for seeing that these orders of mine are carried out.'

At seven in the morning, after returning the dogs to their cages, the Marquis went to Abrenuncio's house. The doctor came to the door in person, for he had no slaves or servants. The Marquis himself uttered the reproach he believed he deserved.

'This is no hour for a visit,' he said.

The doctor, grateful for the horse he had just received, opened his heart. He led him through the courtyard to a shed, all that remained of an old smithy except a ruined forge. The handsome two-year-old sorrel, far from familiar surroundings, seemed restless. Abrenuncio soothed the animal with pats on the cheek while he whispered empty promises in Latin into its ear.

The Marquis told him that the dead horse had been buried in the former garden of the Amor de Dios Hospital, which had been consecrated as a cemetery for the wealthy during the cholera plague. Abrenuncio thanked him for his excessive kindness. As they spoke, he noticed that his visitor stood at a certain distance. The Marquis confessed that he had never had the courage to ride.

'Horses frighten me as much as chickens do,' he said.

'That is too bad, because lack of communication with horses has impeded human progress,' said Abrenuncio. 'If we ever broke down the barriers, we could produce the centaur.'

The interior of the house, illuminated by two windows open to the great sea, was arranged with the excessive fastidiousness of a confirmed bachelor. The atmosphere was permeated with a fragrance of balms, which encouraged belief in the efficacy of medicine. There was a neat and ordered desk and a glass case containing porcelain flasks labeled in Latin. The curative harp, covered by golden dust, was relegated to a corner. Most notable were the books, many of them in Latin, with ornate spines. They were behind glass doors and on open shelves, or arranged with great care on the floor, and the physician walked the narrow paper canyons with the ease of a rhinoceros among the roses. The Marquis was amazed at the number of volumes.

'All knowledge must be in this room,' he said.

'Books are worthless,' Abrenuncio said with good

humor. 'Life has helped me cure the diseases that other doctors cause with their medicines.'

He removed a sleeping cat from the large armchair, which was his, so that the Marquis could sit down. He served him a herbal brew that he prepared on his alchemist's burner and spoke about his medical experiences, until he realized that the Marquis had lost interest. It was true: in a sudden movement he had stood and turned his back, looking through the window at the ill-tempered sea. At last, with his back still turned, he found the courage to begin.

'Doctor,' he murmured.

Abrenuncio had not expected him to speak.

'Hmm?'

'Protected by medical confidentiality, and only for your information, I confess that what they say is true,' said the Marquis in a solemn tone. 'The rabid dog also bit my daughter.'

He looked at the doctor and saw a soul at peace.

'I know,' said the doctor. 'And I suppose that is why you have come here so early.'

'It is,' said the Marquis. And he repeated the question he had already asked about the rabies victim in the hospital: 'What can we do?'

Instead of his brutal response of the previous day, Abrenuncio asked to see Sierva María. That was what the Marquis had come to request. And so they were in agreement, and the carriage was waiting for them at the door.

When they reached the house the Marquis found Bernarda seated at her dressing table, arranging her hair for no one, with the coquetry of those distant years when they made love for the last time, and which he had erased from memory. The room was saturated with the springtime fragrance of her soaps. She saw her husband in the mirror and said without acerbity, 'Who are we to go around giving away horses as presents?'

The Marquis evaded the question. He picked up her everyday tunic from the unmade bed, threw it over Bernarda and with no compassion ordered, 'Get dressed, the doctor is here.'

'God help me,' she said.

'Not for you, although you are in dire need of one,' he said. 'He has come to see the girl.'

'It won't do her any good,' Bernarda said. 'She'll either die or she won't: there's no other possibility.' But curiosity got the better of her. 'Who is he?'

'Abrenuncio,' said the Marquis.

Bernarda was appalled. She preferred to die just as she was, alone and naked, rather than to place her honor in the hands of a grasping Jew. He had been her parents' doctor, and they had repudiated him because he divulged the condition of his patients in order to glorify his diagnoses. The Marquis confronted her.

'Although you do not wish it, and although I wish it even less, you are her mother,' he said. 'On the basis of that sacred right, I ask you to consent to the examination.'

'As far as I'm concerned, you can all do whatever you want,' said Bernarda. 'I'm a dead woman.'

Contrary to expectations, the girl submitted without fuss to a meticulous exploration of her body, displaying the same curiosity she might have shown toward a wind-up toy.

'Doctors see with their hands,' Abrenuncio told her.

Amused, the girl smiled at him for the first time.

The signs of her good health were plain to see, for despite her forlorn air she had a well-proportioned body covered by an almost invisible golden down and showing the first buds of an auspicious flowering. Her teeth were perfect, her eyes clear-sighted, her feet calm, her hands adroit, and each strand of hair was the prelude to a long life. She answered his subtle questions with good humor and a great deal of authority, and one would have had to know her very well to realize that none of her replies was true. She tensed only when the physician discovered the tiny scar on her ankle. Abrenuncio demonstrated his astuteness: 'Did you fall?'

The girl nodded without blinking: 'From the swing.'

The doctor began to speak to himself in Latin. The Marquis interrupted: 'Say it in Spanish.'

I am not talking to you,' said Abrenuncio. 'I think in Low Latin.'

Sierva María was delighted by Abrenuncio's wiles until he put his ear to her chest. Her heart pounded in alarm, and her skin released a livid, icy dew that had a faint onion odor. When he was finished, the doctor gave her an affectionate pat on the cheek.

'You are very brave,' he said.

When he was alone with the Marquis, he told him that the girl knew the dog was rabid. The Marquis did not understand.

'She told you many falsehoods,' he said, 'but that was not one of them.'

'She did not tell me, Señor,' said the doctor. 'Her heart did: it was like a little caged frog.'

The Marquis lingered over the inventory of his daughter's other surprising lies, not with displeasure but with a certain paternal pride. 'Perhaps she will be a poet,' he said. Abrenuncio did not agree that lying was an attribute of the arts.

'The more transparent the writing, the more visible the poetry,' he said.

The only thing he could not interpret was the smell of onions in the girl's perspiration. Since he knew of no connection between any odor and the disease of rabies, he rejected it as a symptom of anything. Caridad del Cobre later revealed to the Marquis that Sierva María had given herself over in secret to the lore of the slaves, who had her chew a paste of *manajú* and placed her naked in the onion cellar to counteract the evil spell of the dog.

Abrenuncio did not sweeten the slightest detail of rabies. 'The first attack is more serious and rapid the deeper the bite and the closer it is to the brain,' he said. He recalled the case of one of his patients who died after five years, although there was some possibility he had contracted a subsequent infection that had gone unnoticed. Rapid scarring meant nothing: after an indeterminate time the scar could become inflamed, open again and suppurate. The agony was so awful that death itself was preferable. The only legal thing one could do then was turn to the Amor de Dios Hospital, where they had Senegalese trained to control heretics and raging maniacs. Otherwise the Marquis himself would have to assume the dreadful burden of keeping the girl chained to her bed until she died.

'In the long history of humankind,' he concluded, 'no hydrophobe has lived to tell the tale.'

The Marquis decided there was no cross, no matter how heavy, that he was not prepared to carry. The girl would die at home. The doctor rewarded him with a look that seemed more pitying than respectful.

'One could expect no less nobility on your part, Señor,' he said. 'And I do not doubt that your soul will have the strength to endure.'

Again he insisted that the prognosis was not alarming. The wound was far from the area of greatest risk, and no one recalled any bleeding. The most probable outcome was that Sierva María would not contract rabies.

'And in the meantime?' asked the Marquis.

'In the meantime,' said Abrenuncio, 'play music for her, fill the house with flowers, have the birds sing, take her to the ocean to see the sunsets, give her everything that can make her happy.' He took his leave with a wave of his hat and the obligatory sentence in Latin. But this time he translated it in honor of the Marquis: 'No medicine cures what happiness cannot.'

Two

No one ever knew how the Marquis had reached a state of such neglect or why he maintained so unharmonious a marriage when his life had been disposed to a peaceful widowerhood. He could have been whatever he wanted to be, given the extraordinary power of his father, the first Marquis, a Knight of the Order of Santiago, a pitiless slave trader and a heartless slave driver, whose king spared him no honors or sinecures and punished none of his crimes.

Ygnacio, his only heir, gave no indications of being anything. He grew up showing undeniable signs of mental retardation, was illiterate until he reached his majority and loved no one. He experienced the first symptom of life at the age of twenty, when he courted and was prepared to marry one of the Divina Pastora inmates whose songs and shouts had been the lullabies of his childhood. Her name was Dulce Olivia. The only child in a family of saddlers to kings, she had been obliged to learn the art of saddle-making so that a tradition almost two centuries old would not die out with her. So unusual an incursion into a man's trade was the explanation given for her losing her reason, and in so drastic a way that teaching her not to eat her own filth was a formidable task. Except for this, it would have been an excellent match for an American-born marquis of limited intelligence.

Dulce Olivia had sharp wits and a strong character and

it was not easy to detect her madness. From the first time he saw her, young Ygnacio could pick her out in the noisy crowd of inmates on the terrace, and that very day they communicated by signs. An expert in the art of paper-folding, she sent him messages in little paper birds. He learned to read and write in order to correspond with her, and this was the beginning of a legitimate passion that no one was willing to understand. The first Marquis was scandalized and ordered his son to make a public denial.

'Not only is it true,' Ygnacio replied, 'but I have her permission to ask for her hand.' And in response to the argument that she was crazy, he countered with one of his own: 'Crazy people are not crazy if one accepts their reasoning.'

His father banished him to his country estates with the authority of lord and master, which he did not deign to exercise. It was a living death. Ygnacio was terrified of all animals except chickens. But on the estates he observed a live chicken at close quarters, imagined it grown to the size of a cow and realized it was a monster much more fearsome than any other on land or sea. He would break into an icy sweat in the darkness and wake at dawn unable to breathe because of the phantasmal silence of the pastures. More than any other danger, the unblinking hunting mastiff that guarded his bedroom unnerved him. He said it himself: 'I live in fear of being alive.' In exile he acquired his lugubrious appearance, cautious manner, contemplative nature, languid behavior, slow speech and a mystic vocation that seemed to condemn him to a cloistered cell.

At the end of his first year of exile he was awakened

by a noise like rivers in flood: the animals on the estate had abandoned their beds and were crossing the fields in absolute silence beneath the full moon. Without making a sound they trampled everything in their path as they moved straight across pastures and canebrakes, torrential streams and flooded marshlands. At their head were the herds of cattle and the work- and saddle-horses, followed by pigs, sheep and barnyard fowl, in a sinister line that disappeared into the night. Even birds of flight, including the pigeons, were leaving. Only the hunting mastiff remained at his post outside the master's bedroom. This marked the beginning of the almost human friendship the Marquis maintained with that dog and with the many mastiffs who succeeded him in the house.

Beside himself with terror on the deserted estate, Ygnacio the Younger renounced his love and submitted to his father's plans. But his father, not satisfied with the sacrifice of love, required in a clause in his will that his son marry the heir of a Spanish grandee. This was how he was joined, in a sumptuous wedding, to Doña Olalla de Mendoza, a very beautiful woman of great and varied talents, whose virginity he kept intact so as not to confer on her even the grace of having a child. For the rest, he continued the life of what he had always been since the day of his birth: a useless bachelor.

Doña Olalla de Mendoza brought him into the world. They attended High Mass, more to be seen than for reasons of faith, she in ruffled skirts and splendid shawls and the starched lace headdress of a white woman from Castille, with an entourage of slave women dressed in silk and covered in gold. Instead of the house slippers that even the most fastidious ladies wore to church she put on high boots of Cordoban leather decorated with pearls. Unlike other distinguished men who favored anachronistic wigs and emerald buttons, the Marquis wore cotton clothing and a soft biretta. His attendance at public events, however, was always a matter of obligation, because he never could conquer his horror of social life.

Doña Olalla had been a student of Scarlatti Domenico in Segovia and had obtained with honors her certificate to teach music and singing in schools and convents. She arrived from Spain with the disassembled parts of a clavichord, which she put together herself, and various string instruments that she played and taught with great virtuosity. She formed an ensemble of novices who sanctified the afternoons in the house with new airs from Italy, France and Spain, and people said they were inspired by the lyricism of the Holy Spirit.

The Marquis seemed unfit for music. It was said, in the French manner, that he had the hands of an artist and the ear of an artilleryman. But from the day the instruments were removed from their crates he was attracted by an Italian lute, the theorbo, because of the strangeness of its double neck, the size of its fingerboard, the number of its strings and the clarity of its voice. Doña Olalla resolved that he would play it as well as she did. They spent the mornings stumbling through exercises under the trees in the orchard, she with patience and love and he with the obstinacy of a stonecutter, until the repentant madrigal surrendered to them without regret.

Music so improved their conjugal harmony that Doña Olalla dared to take the step that was missing. One stormy night, perhaps feigning a dread she did not feel, she went to the bedchamber of her virgin husband.

'I am mistress of half this bed,' she declared, 'and I have come to claim it.'

He stood firm. Convinced she could persuade him by reason or by force, so did she. But life did not give them time. One ninth of November, when they were playing a duet under the orange trees because the air was pure and the sky was high and cloudless, a sudden flash blinded them, a seismic detonation startled them, and Doña Olalla was struck down by lightning.

The horrified city interpreted the tragedy as an explosion of divine wrath in response to some unconfessable sin. The Marquis ordered a queen's funeral, at which he made his first appearance in the black taffeta and waxen color he would wear forever after. When he returned from the cemetery, he was surprised by a storm of little paper birds falling like snow on the orange trees in the orchard. He caught one of them, unfolded it and read: *that lightning bolt was mine.*

Before the nine days of mourning were over he had made a donation to the Church of the lands that sustained the grandeur of his inheritance: a cattle ranch in Mompox and another in Ayapel and 2,000 hectares in Mahates, just two leagues from here, with several herds of riding- and show-horses, a farm and the finest sugar plantation on the Caribbean coast. The legend of his wealth, however, was based on an immense, idle landholding, whose imaginary boundaries, lost in memory beyond the marshes of La Guaripa and the lowlands of La Pureza, extended all the way to the mangrove swamps of Urabá. The only thing he kept was the seignorial mansion with its slave courtyard reduced to a minimum and the sugar plantation at Mahates. He handed over the governance of the house to Dominga de Adviento. He maintained old Neptuno's rank as coachman, which had been granted him by the first Marquis, and put him in charge of the little that remained of the domestic stables.

Alone for the first time in the gloomy mansion of his forebears, he did not sleep well in the darkness because of the congenital fear of American-born nobles that their slaves would murder them in their beds. He would wake with a start, not knowing if the feverish eyes at the transoms were of this world or the next. He would tiptoe to the door, open it with a sudden movement and surprise a slave spying on him through the keyhole. He heard the blacks, naked and smeared with coconut oil to elude capture, slip away with tiger steps along the corridors. Overwhelmed by so many simultaneous fears, he ordered that the lamps be kept burning until dawn, ejected the slaves who, little by little, had been taking over the empty spaces and brought into the house the first mastiffs trained in the arts of war.

The main entrance to the house was closed. The French furnishings, their velvet stinking of dampness, were banished, the Gobelin tapestries and porcelains and masterpieces of the clockmaker's art were sold, and string hammocks were hung in the dismantled bedchambers to fend off the heat. The Marquis did not hear another Mass or go on another retreat, he did not carry the pallium of Our Lord in processions or observe holidays or respect fasts, although he continued to be punctual in paying his tithes to the Church. He took refuge in his hammock, sometimes in the bedroom during the lethargy of August, and almost always under the orange trees in the orchard for his siesta. The madwomen would throw down kitchen scraps and shout tender obscenities at him, but when the government offered him the courtesy of moving the lunatic asylum, he objected out of gratitude to its inmates.

Conquered by the rebuffs of the man she had wooed, Dulce Olivia found consolation in nostalgia for what had never been. Whenever she could she would escape from Divina Pastora through breaches in the orchard. She tamed the hunting mastiffs and made them her own with the food of her chaste love, and devoted the hours when she should have been sleeping to caring for the house she never had, sweeping it with brooms made of sweet basil for good luck and hanging strings of garlic in the bedrooms to frighten away mosquitoes. Dominga de Adviento, whose right hand left nothing to chance, died without ever discovering why the corridors were cleaner at dawn than they had been the night before and why the things she had arranged one way were in a different order the next morning. The Marquis had been a widower for less than a year when he discovered Dulce Olivia in the kitchen for the first time, scrubbing pots and pans that she believed the slave women had left dirty.

'I did not think you would dare so much,' he said.

'That's because you're still the same poor devil you always were,' she replied.

And so they resumed a forbidden friendship that at one time, at least, had resembled love. They would talk until dawn, without illusions or rancor, like an old married couple condemned to routine. They thought they were happy, and perhaps they were, until one of them said one word too many, or took one step too few, and the night rotted into a battle between Vandals that demoralized the mastiffs. Then everything would go back to the beginning, and for a long while Dulce Olivia would not return to the house.

The Marquis confessed to her that his contempt for the goods of this world and the changes in his way of life were the result not of devotion, but of the fear caused by his abrupt loss of faith when he saw his wife's body charred by lightning. Dulce Olivia offered to console him. She promised to be his submissive slave in both the kitchen and the bed. He did not yield.

'I will never marry again,' he vowed.

Before the year was out, however, he had been married in secret to Bernarda Cabrera, the daughter of one of his father's former overseers who had made a fortune in imported foods. They had met when Bernarda's father sent her to the house with the pickled herring and black olives that were Doña Olalla's weakness, and when she died, Bernarda continued to bring them to the Marquis. One afternoon she found him in the hammock in the orchard and read the destiny written on the palm of his left hand. The Marquis was so impressed by her accuracy that he kept sending for her at siesta time even when he had nothing to buy, but two months passed and he made no move of any kind. And so she did it for him. She stormed the hammock, mounted him, gagged him with the skirts of the djellaba he was wearing and left him exhausted. Then she revived him with an ardor and skill he could not have imagined in the meager pleasures of his solitary lovemaking and without glory deprived him of his virginity. He was fifty-two years old and she was twenty-three, but age was the least pernicious of the differences between them.

They continued to make hurried, heartless siesta love in the evangelical shade of the orange trees. The madwomen encouraged them from the terraces with indecent songs and celebrated their triumphs with stadium ovations. Before the Marquis was aware of the dangers that pursued him, Bernarda woke him from his stupor with the news that she was in the second month of pregnancy. She reminded him that she was not a black but the daughter of an astute Indian and a white woman from Castille, and the only needle that could mend her honor was formal matrimony. He held her off until one siesta when her father knocked at the main door, an ancient harquebus slung over his shoulder. He was slow of speech and gentle of manner, and he handed the weapon to the Marquis without looking him in the face.

'Do you know what this is, Señor Marquis?' he asked.

The Marquis did not know what to do with the weapon he was holding.

'If I am not mistaken, I believe it is a harquebus,' he said. And he asked with genuine bewilderment, 'What do you use it for?'

'To defend myself against pirates, Señor,' said the Indian, still not looking him in the face. 'I have brought it now in the event Your Excellency wishes to do me the honor of killing me before I kill you.'

Then he looked straight at him. His narrow eyes were sad and silent, but the Marquis understood what they did not say. He returned the harquebus and invited him in to celebrate their arrangement. Two days later the priest of a nearby church officiated at the wedding, which was attended by her parents and both their sponsors. When it was over, Sagunta appeared out of nowhere and crowned the bride and groom with the wreaths of happiness.

One morning, during a late rainstorm and under the sign of Sagittarius, Sierva María de Todos los Ángeles was born, premature and puny. She looked like a bleached tadpole, and the umbilical cord wrapped around her neck was strangling her.

'It's a girl,' said the midwife. 'But it won't live.'

That was when Dominga de Adviento promised her saints that if they granted the girl the grace of life, her hair would not be cut until her wedding night. No sooner had she made the promise than the girl began to cry. Dominga de Adviento sang out in jubilation, 'She will be a saint!' The Marquis, who saw her for the first time when she was bathed and dressed, was less prescient.

'She will be a whore,' he said. 'If God gives her life and health.'

The girl, daughter of an aristocrat and a commoner, had the childhood of a foundling. Her mother hated her from the moment she nursed her for the first and only time and then refused to keep the baby with her for fear she would kill her. Dominga de Adviento suckled her, baptized her in Christ and consecrated her to Olokun, a Yoruban deity of indeterminate sex whose face is presumed to be so dreadful it is seen only in dreams and always hidden by a mask. Transplanted to the courtyard of the slaves, Sierva María learned to dance before she could speak, learned three African languages at the same time, learned to drink rooster's blood before breakfast and to glide past Christians unseen and unheard, like an incorporeal being. Dominga de Adviento surrounded her with a jubilant court of black slave women, mestiza maids and Indian errand girls, who bathed her in propitiatory waters, purified her with the verbena of Yemayá and tended the torrent of hair, which fell to her waist by the time she was five, as if it were a rosebush. Over time the slave women hung the beads of various gods around her neck, until she was wearing sixteen necklaces.

Bernarda had seized control of the house with a firm hand while the Marquis vegetated in the orchard. Shielded by the powers of the first Marquis, she set about restoring the fortune given away by her husband. In his day, the first Marquis had obtained licenses to sell 5,000 slaves in eight years, agreeing to import two barrels of flour for each black. Making use of masterful fraud and the venality of the customs agents, he sold the mandated flour but also smuggled and sold 3,000 more slaves than he had contracted for, which made him the most successful individual trader of his century.

It was Bernarda who realized that the profitable business was not slaves but flour, although in reality the greatest profits lay in her incredible powers of persuasion. With a single license to import 1,000 slaves in four years, and three barrels of flour for each black, she made the deal of a lifetime: she sold the contracted number of slaves, but instead of 3,000 barrels of flour she imported 12,000. It was the largest smuggling operation of the century.

During this period she spent half her time at the Mahates sugar plantation, where she established the center of her business affairs, since the proximity of the Great Magdalena River allowed for every kind of traffic with the interior of the vice-regency. Occasional reports of her prosperity reached the house of the Marquis, but she rendered accounts to no one. When she spent time here, even before her crises, she seemed like another caged mastiff. Dominga de Adviento said it best: 'Her ass was too big for her body.'

When her slave woman died, and the splendid bedroom of the first Marquise was prepared for her, Sierva María occupied a stable position in the house for the first time. A tutor was named to give her lessons in Peninsular Spanish and impart some notion of arithmetic and the natural sciences. He tried to teach her to read and write. She refused, she said, because she could not understand the letters. A lay teacher introduced her to an appreciation of music. The girl showed interest and good taste but did not have the patience to learn an instrument. The teacher resigned in consternation and said, as she took her leave of the Marquis, 'It is not that the girl is unfit for everything; it is that she is not of this world.'

Bernarda had wanted to quiet her own rancorous feelings toward the girl, but it soon became evident that the fault lay not in one or the other but in the very nature of each. She had lived with her heart in her mouth ever since she discovered a certain phantasmal quality in her daughter. She trembled at the mere memory of the times she would turn around and find herself face to face with the inscrutable eyes of the languid creature in filmy tulle, whose untamed hair now reached to the back of her knees. 'Girl!' she would shout. 'I forbid you to look at me that way!' When she was most involved in her business affairs, she would feel on the back of her neck the sibilant breath of a snake lying in ambush and recoil in terror.

'Girl!' she would shout. 'Make a noise before you come in!'

And the girl would heighten her fear with a string of Yoruban curses. At night it was worse, because Bernarda would wake with a start, sensing that someone had touched her, and there was the girl at the foot of the bed, watching her as she slept. Her attempt to tie a cowbell around Sierva María's wrist failed because the girl's movements were so stealthy it did not make a sound. 'The only thing white about that child is her color,' her mother would say. This was so true that the girl changed her name to an African name of her own invention: María Mandinga.

Their relationship reached a crisis when Bernarda woke in the small hours of the morning, dying of thirst brought on by excesses of cacao, and found one of Sierva María's dolls at the bottom of the large water jar. She did not think it was really a simple doll floating in the water but something horrifying: a murdered doll.

Convinced that Sierva María had cast an evil African spell on her, she decided that the two of them could not live in the same house. The Marquis attempted a timid mediation, and she cut him off: 'It's her or me.' And so Sierva María returned to the slave women's shack, even when her mother was at the sugar plantation. She remained as reticent as when she was born and as illiterate.

But Bernarda was no better off. She had tried to hold on to Judas Iscariote by becoming like him and in less than two years she lost her bearings in her business and even her life. She would dress him as a Nubian pirate, as the Ace of Clubs, as King Melchior, and take him to the poor districts, above all when the galleons were anchored in the bay and the city went on a binge that lasted half a year. Taverns and brothels were improvised in outlying districts for the merchants who came from Lima, Portobelo, Havana or Veracruz to contend for goods and merchandise from all over the discovered world. One night, staggering with drink in a tavern for galley slaves, Judas came up to Bernarda in a very mysterious way.

'Open your mouth and close your eyes,' he said.

She did, and he placed a tablet of the magic chocolate from Oaxaca on her tongue. Bernarda recognized the taste and spat it out, for she had felt a special aversion to cacao ever since her childhood. Judas convinced her it was a sacred substance that brought joy to life, enhanced physical prowess, raised the spirits and strengthened sexuality.

Bernarda exploded in laughter.

'If that were true,' she said, 'the good Sisters of Santa Clara would be fighting bulls.'

She was already addicted to fermented honey, which she had consumed with her schoolfriends before she was married and still consumed, not only by mouth but through all five senses in the sultry air of the sugar plantation. With Judas she learned to chew tobacco and coca leaves mixed with ashes of the *yarumo* tree, like the Indians in the Sierra Nevada. In the taverns she experimented with cannabis from India, turpentine from Cyprus, peyote from Real de Catorce and, at least once, opium from the Nao of China brought by Filipino traffickers. But she did not turn a deaf ear to Judas's proclamation in favor of cacao. After trying all the rest, she recognized its virtues and preferred it to everything else. Judas became a thief, a pimp, an occasional sodomite, all out of sheer depravity because he lacked for nothing. One ill-fated night, in front of Bernarda, with only his bare hands, he fought three galley slaves in a dispute over cards and was beaten to death with a chair.

Bernarda took refuge on the sugar plantation. The house was left to drift, and if it did not sink then, it was because of the masterful hand of Dominga de Adviento, who, in the end, raised Sierva María as her gods willed. The Marquis knew next to nothing of his wife's downfall. Rumors from the plantation said that she was living in a state of delirium, that she talked to herself, that she selected the best-endowed slaves and shared them in Roman orgies with her former schoolmates. The fortune that came to her by water left by water, and she was at the mercy of the skins of honey and sacks of cacao that she kept hidden in various places so she would lose no time when her relentless longings pursued her. The only security she had left were two urns filled with gold doubloons, pieces of one hundred and pieces of four, which she had buried under her bed in the days of plenty. Her deterioration was so great that not even her husband recognized her when, after three uninterrupted years at the sugar plantation, she returned from Mahates for the last time, not long before the dog bit Sierva María.

By the middle of March the risk of rabies seemed to have been averted. The Marquis, grateful for his good fortune, resolved to rectify the past and win the girl's heart with the prescription for happiness recommended by Abrenuncio. He devoted all his time to her. He tried to learn to comb and braid her hair. He tried to teach her to be a real white, to revive for her his failed dreams of an American-born noble, to suppress her fondness for pickled iguana and armadillo stew. He attempted almost everything except asking himself whether this was the way to make her happy.

Abrenuncio continued to visit the house. It was not easy for him to communicate with the Marquis but he was intrigued by his lack of awareness in an outpost of the world intimidated by the Holy Office. And so the months of hot weather passed, Abrenuncio talking without being heard beneath the flowering orange trees, and the Marquis rotting in his hammock at a distance of 1,300 nautical leagues from a king who had never heard his name. During one of these visits they were interrupted by a baleful lament from Bernarda.

Abrenuncio was alarmed. The Marquis pretended to be deaf, but the next groan was so heartrending he could not ignore it. 'That person, whoever it is, needs help,' said Abrenuncio.

'That person is my second wife,' said the Marquis.

'Well, her liver is diseased,' said Abrenuncio.

'How do you know?'

'Because she groans with her mouth open,' said the doctor.

He pushed her door open without knocking and tried to see Bernarda in the darkened room, but she was not in the bed. He called her by name, and she did not answer. Then he opened the window, and the metallic light of four o'clock revealed her, naked and sprawled in a cross on the floor, enveloped in the glow of her lethal gases. Her skin had the pale gray color of full-blown dyspepsia. She raised her head, blinded by the sudden brilliance streaming in the open window and could not recognize the doctor with the light behind him. One glance was all he needed to know her destiny.

'The piper is demanding to be paid, my dear,' he said.

He explained that there was still time to save her, but only if she submitted to an emergency treatment to purify her blood. Then Bernarda recognized him, struggled into a sitting position and let loose a string of obscenities. An impassive Abrenuncio endured them as he closed the window again. He left the room, stopped beside the Marquis's hammock and made a more specific prognosis: 'The Señora Marquise will die on the fifteenth of September at the latest, if she does not hang herself from the rafters first.'

Unmoved, the Marquis said, 'The only problem is that the fifteenth of September is so far away.'

He continued with the prescription of happiness for Sierva María. From San Lázaro Hill they observed the fatal swamps to the east and to the west the enormous red sun as it sank into a flaming sea. She asked what was on the other side of the ocean, and he replied: 'The world.' For each of his gestures he discovered an unexpected resonance in the girl. One afternoon they saw the Galleon Fleet appear on the horizon, its sails full to bursting.

The city was transformed. Father and daughter were entertained by puppet shows, by fire-eaters, by the countless fairground attractions coming into port during that April of good omen. In two months Sierva María learned more about white people's ways than she ever had before. In his effort to transform her, the Marquis also became a different man, and in so drastic a manner that it did not seem an alteration in his personality as much as a change in his very nature.

The house was filled with every kind of wind-up ballerina, music box and mechanical clock displayed in the fairs of Europe. The Marquis dusted off the Italian theorbo. He restrung it, tuned it with a perseverance that could be understood only as love and once again accompanied the songs of the past, sung with the good voice and bad ear that neither years nor troubled memories had changed. This was when she asked him whether it was true that love conquered all, as the songs said.

'It is true,' he replied, 'but you would do well not to believe it.'

Pleased by these good tidings, the Marquis began to consider a trip to Seville so that Sierva María could recover from her silent sorrows and finish learning about the world. The dates and itinerary had already been arranged when Caridad del Cobre woke him from his siesta with brutal news: 'Señor, my poor girl is turning into a dog.'

Called in for the emergency, Abrenuncio refuted the popular superstition that the victims of rabies became identical to the animal that had bitten them. He confirmed that the girl had a slight fever, and although this was considered a disease in itself and not a symptom of other ailments, he did not disregard it. He warned the grief-stricken nobleman that the girl was not safe from any illness, for the bite of a dog, rabid or not, offered no protection against anything else. As always, the only recourse was to wait.

The Marquis asked him, 'Is that all you can tell me?'

'Science has not given me the means to tell you anything

else,' the physician replied with the same acerbity. 'But if you have no faith in me, you still have another recourse: put your trust in God.'

The Marquis did not understand.

'I would have sworn you were an unbeliever,' he said.

The doctor did not even turn to look at him. 'I only wish I were, Señor.'

The Marquis put his trust not in God but in anything that might offer some hope. The city had three other physicians, six pharmacists, eleven barber-surgeons and countless magical healers and masters of the arts of sorcery, although the Inquisition had condemned 1,300 of them to a variety of punishments over the past fifty years and burned seven at the stake. A young physician from Salamanca opened Sierva María's closed wound and applied caustic poultices to draw out the rank humors. Another attempted to achieve the same end with leeches on her back. A barber-surgeon bathed the wound in her own urine, and another had her drink it. At the end of two weeks she had been subjected to two herbal baths and two emollient enemas a day and was brought to the brink of death with potions of natural antimony and other fatal concoctions.

The fever subsided, but no one dared proclaim that rabies had been averted. Sierva María felt as if she were dying. At first she had resisted with her pride intact but after two fruitless weeks she had a fiery ulcer on her ankle, her body was scalded by mustard plasters and blistering poultices and the skin on her stomach was raw. She had suffered everything: vertigo, convulsions, spasms, deliriums, looseness of the bowels and bladder; and she rolled on the floor howling in pain and fury. Even the boldest healers left her to her fate, convinced she was mad or possessed by demons. The Marquis had lost all hope when Sagunta appeared with the key of Saint Hubert.

It was the end. Sagunta stripped off her sheets, smeared herself with Indian ointments and rubbed her body against the body of the naked girl. She fought back with her hands and feet despite her extreme weakness, and Sagunta subdued her by force. Bernarda heard their demented screams from her room. She ran to see what was going on and found Sierva María kicking in a rage on the floor, and Sagunta on top of her, wrapped in the copper flood of the girl's hair and bellowing the prayer of Saint Hubert. She whipped them both with the clews of her hammock. First on the floor, where they huddled against the surprise attack, and then pursuing them from corner to corner until she was out of breath.

The bishop of the diocese, Don Toribio de Cáceres y Virtudes, alarmed at the public scandal caused by Sierva María's vicissitudes and ravings, sent for the Marquis but did not specify a reason, a date or a time, which was interpreted as an indication of utmost urgency. The Marquis overcame his uncertainty and paid an unannounced visit that same day.

The Bishop had assumed his ministry when the Marquis was already withdrawn from public life, and they had never met. He was, moreover, a man assailed by poor health; his stentorian body permitted him to do very little on his own and was corroded by a malignant asthma that put his faith to the test. He had not been present at numerous public events where his absence was unthinkable, and at the few he did attend he maintained an aloofness that over time was turning him into an unreal being.

The Marquis had seen him on a few occasions, always at a distance and in public, but the memory he had of the Bishop was a Mass at which he officiated wearing a pallium and was carried in a sedan chair by government dignitaries. Because of his huge body and the extravagant richness of his vestments, at first glance he had seemed nothing more than a colossal old man, but his clean-shaven face, with its precise features and unusual green eyes, preserved an ageless beauty intact. High in the sedan chair, he had the magical aura of a Supreme Pontiff, and those who knew him at closer quarters sensed the same thing in the brilliance of his learning and his consciousness of power.

The palace where he lived was the oldest in the city and had two stories of vast, ruined spaces, although the Bishop occupied less than half a floor. It was adjacent to the cathedral, and the two buildings shared a cloister with blackened arches and a courtyard where a crumbling cistern was surrounded by desert scrub. Even its imposing façade of carved stone and great entrances made of single timbers revealed the ravages of neglect.

The Marquis was received at the main door by an Indian deacon. He distributed meager alms to the crowd of beggars crawling in front of the portico, and entered the cool shadows of the interior just as the enormous tolling of four o'clock sounded in the cathedral and resounded in his belly. The central corridor was so dark that he followed after the deacon without seeing him and considered each step before taking it to avoid stumbling over ill-placed statues and debris that blocked the way. At the end of the corridor was a small anteroom where a transom provided more light. The deacon stopped here, asked the Marquis to have a seat and wait and then walked through the door into an adjoining room. The Marquis remained standing and looked at a large oil portrait, hung on the long wall, of a young soldier in the dress uniform of the King's Cadets. Only when he read the bronze plaque on the frame did he realize it was a portrait of the Bishop in his youth.

The deacon opened the door to ask him in, and the Marquis did not have to move to see the Bishop again, forty years older than in his portrait. Even overcome by asthma and undone by the heat, he was much larger and more imposing than people claimed. The perspiration streamed off his body, and he rocked at a snail's pace in a chair from the Philippines, barely moving a palm fan back and forth as he leaned forward to ease his breathing. He was dressed in peasant sandals and a tunic of coarse linen with patches worn thin by abuses of soap. The sincerity of his poverty was evident at first glance. Most notable, however, was the purity of his eyes, understandable only as a privilege of the soul. He stopped rocking as soon as he saw the Marquis in the doorway and waved the fan in an affectionate gesture.

'Come in, Ygnacio,' he said. 'My house is yours.'

The Marquis wiped his perspiring hands on his trousers, walked through the door and found himself under a canopy of yellow bellflowers and hanging ferns on an outdoor terrace that overlooked all the church towers, the red-tile roofs of the principal houses, the dovecotes drowsing in the heat, the military fortifications outlined against the glass sky, the burning sea. The Bishop extended his soldier's hand in a meaningful way, and the Marquis kissed his ring.

Asthma made his breathing heavy and stony, and his phrases were interrupted by inopportune sighs and a harsh, brief cough, but nothing could affect his eloquence. He established an immediate, easy exchange of trivial commonplaces. Sitting across from him, the Marquis was grateful for this consolatory preamble, so rich and protracted that they were taken aback when the bells tolled five. More than a sound, it was a vibration that made the afternoon light tremble and filled the sky with startled pigeons.

'It is horrible,' said the Bishop. 'Each hour resonates deep inside me like an earthquake.'

The phrase surprised the Marquis, for he had responded with the same thought at four o'clock. It seemed a natural coincidence to the Bishop. 'Ideas do not belong to anyone,' he said. With his index finger he sketched a series of continuous circles in the air and concluded, 'They fly around up there like the angels.'

A nun in his domestic service brought in a decanter of thick, strong wine with chopped fruit and a basin of steaming water that filled the air with a medicinal odor. The Bishop closed his eyes and inhaled the vapor, and when he emerged from his ecstasy he was another man: the absolute master of his authority.

'We had you come,' he told the Marquis, 'because we know you are in need of God and pretend not to notice.'

His voice had lost its organ tonalities, and his eyes had recovered their earthly light. The Marquis drank half a glass of wine in one swallow to give himself courage.

'Your Grace should know that I am burdened by the greatest misfortune a human being can suffer,' he said with disarming humility. 'I no longer believe.'

'We know, my son,' the Bishop answered without surprise. 'How could we not know!'

He said this with a certain joy, for he too, as a King's Cadet in Morocco, had lost his faith at the age of twenty, surrounded by the din of battle. 'It was the thundering certainty that God had ceased to exist,' he said. In terror he had dedicated himself to a life of prayer and penitence.

'Until God took pity on me and showed me the path of my vocation,' he concluded. 'What is essential, therefore, is not that you no longer believe, but that God continues to believe in you. And regarding that there can be no doubt, for it is He in His infinite diligence who has enlightened us so that we may offer you this consolation.'

'I have tried to endure my misfortune in silence,' said the Marquis.

'Well, you have in no way succeeded,' said the Bishop. 'It is an open secret that your poor child rolls on the floor in obscene convulsions, howling the gibberish of idolaters. Are these not the unequivocal symptoms of demonic possession?'

The Marquis was aghast.

'What do you mean?'

'That one of the demon's numerous deceptions is to take on the appearance of a foul disease in order to enter an innocent body,' he said. 'And once he is inside, no human power is capable of making him leave.'

The Marquis explained the medical alterations in the bite, but the Bishop always found an explanation that favored his position. He asked a question, although there was no doubt he already knew the answer, 'Do you know who Abrenuncio is?'

'He was the first doctor to see the girl,' said the Marquis.

'I wanted to hear it from your own lips,' said the Bishop.

He rang a little bell that he kept by his hand, and a priest in his mid-thirties appeared with the suddenness of a genie liberated from a bottle. The Bishop introduced him as Father Cayetano Delaura, nothing more, and asked him to sit down. He wore a simple cassock because of the heat and sandals like those of the Bishop. He was intense and pale, and had spirited eyes and deep black hair with a streak of white at his forehead. His rapid breathing and feverish hands did not seem those of a happy man.

'What do we know about Abrenuncio?' the Bishop asked him.

Father Delaura did not have to think before answering.

'Abrenuncio de Sa Pereira Cao,' he said, as if spelling out the name. And then he turned to the Marquis. 'Have you noticed, Señor Marquis, that his last family name means "dog" in the language of the Portuguese?'

In actual fact, Delaura continued, it was not known whether that was his real name. According to the records of the Holy Office, he was a Portuguese Jew expelled from the Peninsula and sheltered here by a grateful governor whom he had cured of a two-pound hernia with the purifying waters of Turbaco. He spoke of his magical prescriptions, of the pride with which he foretold death, of his probable pederasty, of his libertine readings, of his life without God. Nevertheless, the only concrete charge brought against him was that he had resurrected a tailor in the district of Getsemaní. Serious testimony had been obtained to the effect that the man was already in his shroud and coffin when Abrenuncio ordered him to rise. It was fortunate that the resurrected tailor himself stated before the tribunal of the Holy Office that at no time had he lost consciousness. 'That saved Abrenuncio from the stake,' said Delaura. He concluded by recalling the incident of the horse that had died on San Lázaro Hill and been buried in holy ground.

'He loved it as if it were a human being,' the Marquis interceded.

'It was an affront to our faith, Señor Marquis,' said Delaura. 'Hundred-year-old horses are not the work of God.'

The Marquis was alarmed that a private joke had reached the archives of the Holy Office. He attempted a timid defense: 'Abrenuncio has a loose tongue, but in all humility I believe there is a good distance between that and heresy.' The discussion would have become bitter and endless if the Bishop had not returned them to the question at hand.

'No matter what the physicians may claim,' he said, 'rabies in humans is often one of the many snares of the Enemy.'

The Marquis did not understand. The Bishop gave him so dramatic an explanation that it seemed the prelude to eternal damnation.

'It is fortunate,' he concluded, 'that although your daughter's body may be lost forever, God has provided us with the means to save her soul.'

The oppressiveness of twilight filled the world. The Marquis saw the first star in the mauve sky and thought of his daughter, alone in the wretched house, dragging her abused foot through the botched cures of the healers. With his natural modesty he asked, 'What should I do?'

The Bishop told him point by point. He authorized him to use his name at every step of the way, above all at the Convent of Santa Clara, where he was to confine the girl without delay.

'Put her in our hands,' he concluded. 'God will do the rest.'

The Marquis took his leave more troubled than when he arrived. From the window of his carriage he contemplated the desolate streets, the children playing naked in the puddles, the garbage scattered by the turkey buzzards. The carriage turned the corner and he saw the ocean, always in its place, and he was assailed by uncertainty.

He reached the darkened house as the Angelus was ringing and for the first time since the death of Doña Olalla he said the prayer aloud: '*The angel of the Lord announced to Mary.*' The strings of the theorbo resonated in the shadows as if at the bottom of a pond. The Marquis felt his way, following the sound of the music to his daughter's bedroom. There she was, seated on her dressing-table chair in a white tunic, her unbound hair falling to the floor, playing an elementary exercise she had learned from him. Unless a miracle had occurred, he could not believe she was the same girl he had left at noon, prostrated by the cruelty of the healers. It was a fleeting illusion. Sierva María became aware of his presence, stopped playing and fell back into her affliction.

He stayed with her the entire night. He assisted in the

ritual of the bedroom with all the clumsiness of a borrowed father. He put her nightdress on backward, and she had to take it off and put it on again the right way. He had not seen her naked before and he was saddened by her ribs so close to the skin, her little button nipples, her tender down. A burning halo surrounded the inflamed ankle. As he helped her into bed, the girl continued her solitary suffering with an almost inaudible moan, and he was shaken by the certainty that he was helping her to die.

For the first time since losing his faith he felt the urge to pray. He went to the oratory, trying with all his strength to recover the god who had forsaken him, but to no avail: disbelief is more resistant than faith because it is sustained by the senses. He heard the girl cough several times in the cool air of the small hours and he returned to her bedroom. On the way he saw that Bernarda's door was ajar. He pushed it open, moved by the need to share his doubts. She was lying face up on the floor, and her snores were deafening. The Marquis remained in the doorway, his hand on the latch, and did not wake her. He said to no one, 'Your life for hers.' And made an immediate correction: 'Both our shit lives for hers, damn it!'

The girl was sleeping. The Marquis saw her motionless and pale and wondered if he preferred to see her dead or suffering the torment of rabies. He adjusted the mosquito netting so the bats would not drain her blood, he covered her so she would not cough and he kept watch next to the bed, feeling the new joy of knowing he loved her as he had never loved in this world. Then he made the decision of his life without consulting God or anyone else. At four in the morning, when Sierva María opened her eyes, she saw him sitting next to her bed.

'It is time for us to go,' said the Marquis.

The girl got up with no further explanations. The Marquis helped her dress for the occasion. He looked in the chest for velvet slippers so the stiff counter of her boot would not chafe her ankle, and happened to find a ball gown that had belonged to his mother when she was a girl. The dress was faded and stained with age but clearly had not been worn twice. Now, almost a century later, the Marquis put it on Sierva María, over her Santería necklaces and baptism scapular. The gown was a little tight and that somehow made it seem older. In the chest he also found a hat with colored ribbons that had nothing to do with the dress. The fit was perfect. Then he packed a small valise with a nightgown, a comb with teeth narrow enough to root out lice eggs and her grandmother's small breviary with gold hinges and mother-of-pearl covers.

It was Palm Sunday. The Marquis took Sierva María to five-o'clock Mass, and she was willing to accept the blessed palm frond without knowing what it was for. As they drove away in the carriage, they saw the sunrise. The Marquis occupied the principal seat, holding the little valise on his knees, and the imperturbable girl sat across from him, looking out the window at the last streets of her twelve-year-old life. She had not expressed the slightest interest in knowing where she was being taken so early in the morning, dressed like mad Queen Juana and wearing the hat of a harlot. After long meditation, the Marquis asked, 'Do you know who God is?'

The girl shook her head no.

There was lightning and distant thunder on the horizon,

the sky was lowering and the ocean surly. They turned a corner and there stood the Convent of Santa Clara, white and solitary, with three floors of blue window blinds facing the rubbish heap of a beach. The Marquis pointed with his finger. 'There it is,' he said. And then he pointed to his left. 'You will see the ocean all day from the windows.' Since the girl took no notice, he gave the only explanation he would ever give her of her destiny: 'You are going to spend a few days with the good Sisters of Santa Clara.'

Because it was Palm Sunday, more beggars than usual were at the entrance with its turnstile gate. Some lepers who were arguing with them over kitchen scraps also rushed toward the Marquis, their hands extended. He distributed meager alms, one coin to each of them until he had no more *cuartillos* left. The nun who guarded the gate saw him in his black taffetas, and the girl dressed like a queen, and she made her way through the crowd to attend to them. The Marquis explained that he was bringing Sierva María by order of the Bishop. The gatekeeper did not doubt it, because of the manner in which he spoke. She examined the girl and removed her hat.

'Hats are forbidden here,' she said.

The nun kept it. The Marquis also tried to hand her the valise, but she would not accept it: 'She won't need anything.'

The girl's braid had not been pinned up with care and it unrolled almost to the ground. The gatekeeper did not believe it was real. The Marquis attempted to roll it again. The girl brushed him aside and arranged her own hair unassisted, and with a skill that surprised the gatekeeper.

'It has to be cut,' she said.

'It is pledged to the Blessed Virgin until the day she marries,' said the Marquis.

The gatekeeper accepted his reasoning. She took the girl by the hand, without giving her time to say goodbye, and passed her through the turnstile. Since her ankle hurt when she walked, the girl took off her left slipper. The Marquis watched her move away, favoring her bare foot and holding the slipper in her hand. He hoped in vain that in a rare moment of compassion she would turn to look at him. The last memory he had of Sierva María was her crossing the gallery in the garden, dragging her painful foot, and disappearing into the pavilion of those interred in life.

Three

The convent of Santa Clara faced the sea and had three floors of innumerable identical windows and a gallery of semicircular arches surrounding a dark, overgrown garden. There was a stone path through the banana trees and wild ferns, a slender palm that had grown higher than the flat roofs in its search for light and a colossal tree with vanilla vines and strings of orchids hanging from its branches. Beneath the tree a cistern of stagnant water had a rusted iron rim on which captive macaws performed like circus acrobats.

The garden divided the convent into two separate wings. To the right were the three floors occupied by those interred in life, where the gasp of the undertow at the cliffs and the prayers and canticles of the canonical hours almost never penetrated. This wing communicated with the chapel by means of an interior door that permitted the cloistered nuns to enter the chancel without passing through the public nave, and hear Mass and sing behind a latticed jalousie through which they could see and not be seen. The beautiful coffered ceiling of noble woods, repeated throughout the convent, had been built by a Spanish artisan who devoted half his life to the work in exchange for the right to be buried in a vaulted niche of the high altar. There he was, crowded behind the marble slabs along with almost two centuries of abbesses and bishops and other eminent personages.

When Sierva María entered the convent, the cloistered

nuns numbered eighty-two Spanishwomen, all with their own servants, and thirty-six American-born daughters of the great viceregal families. After taking their vows of poverty, silence and chastity, their only communication with the outside world was a rare visit held in the locutory, where wooden jalousies admitted voices but not light. The locutory was situated next to the turnstile gate, and its use was regulated, restricted and always required the presence of a chaperone.

To the left of the garden were the schools, every kind of workshop and a large population of novices and female teachers of handicrafts. The service building was located here, with its enormous kitchen and wood-burning stoves, a butchering shop and a great bread oven. At the rear was a courtyard, always flooded with dirty wash-water, where several families of slaves lived together, and beyond that were the stables, a goat pen, the pigsty, the garden and the beehives, where everything needed for the good life was raised and grown.

Last of all, as far away as possible and abandoned by the hand of God, stood a solitary pavilion that had been used as a prison by the Inquisition for sixty-eight years and still served the same purpose for Clarissans gone astray. It was in the farthest cell of this forgotten corner where they would lock Sierva María ninety-three days after she had been bitten by the dog and showed no symptoms of rabies.

At the end of the corridor the gatekeeper who had led her by the hand saw a novice who was going to the kitchens and asked her to take Sierva María to the Abbess. The novice thought it imprudent to subject so languid and well-dressed a girl to the clamor of the kitchens and she left her sitting on one of the stone benches in the garden, planning to return for her later. But on her way back she forgot.

Two novices walked past Sierva María, became interested in her necklaces and rings and asked her who she was. She did not reply. They asked her whether she knew Spanish, and it was as if they were talking to a corpse.

'She's a deaf-mute,' said the younger novice.

'Or German,' said the other.

The younger one began to treat her as if she lacked all her senses. She unrolled the braid that Sierva María had wound at her neck and measured it. 'Almost four spans,' she said, convinced the girl could not hear her. She began to undo the braid but was intimidated by a look. The novice stared back and stuck out her tongue.

'You have the eyes of the devil,' she said.

She removed one of the girl's rings and met no resistance, but when the other novice tried to take her necklaces, Sierva María coiled like a viper and bit her on the hand with perfect, unhesitating aim. The novice ran off to rinse away the blood.

The singing of Terce began just as Sierva María stood to take a drink from the cistern. She was frightened and returned to the bench without drinking, but went back when she realized it was the sound of nuns singing. She pushed away the skim of rotting leaves with a deft movement of the hand and drank her fill from her cupped palm, not bothering to remove the water worms. Then she urinated behind the tree, squatting and holding a stick at the ready to defend herself against abusive animals and predatory men, just as Dominga de Adviento had taught her to do.

A short while later two black slave women came by, recognized the Santería necklaces and spoke to her in Yoruban. The girl's eager reply was in the same language. Since no one knew why she was there, the slaves took her to the tumultuous kitchen, where the servants welcomed her with jubilation. Then someone noticed the wound on her ankle and wanted to know what had happened. 'My mother did it with a knife,' the girl said. When they asked her what she was called, she gave them her black name: María Mandinga.

She had recovered her world. She helped slit the throat of a goat that struggled against dying and cut out its eyes and sliced off its testicles, which were the parts she liked best. She played diabolo with the adults in the kitchen and the children in the courtyard and won every game. She sang in Yoruban, Congolese and Mandingo, and even those who did not understand listened to her, enthralled. For lunch she ate a dish of the goat's eyes and testicles cooked in lard and seasoned with burning spices.

By this time the entire convent knew the girl was there except Josefa Miranda, the Abbess, a lean, hard woman whose narrowness of mind was a family trait. She had been brought up in Burgos, in the shadow of the Holy Office, but her talent for command and the rigor of her prejudices came from within and had always been hers. Two capable nuns served as her vicars, but they were unnecessary because she took charge of everything, with no help from anyone.

Her rancor toward the local Bishopric had begun almost one hundred years before her birth. As in other great historical disputes, the initial cause was a minor disagreement over financial and jurisdictional matters between the Clarissan sisters and the Franciscan bishop. Finding him intransigent, the nuns obtained the support of the civil government, and this was the start of a war that at one point became a free-for-all.

Backed by other communities, the Bishop imposed a state of siege on the convent in order to starve it into submission and decreed the *Cessatio a Divinis*: in other words, the cessation of all religious services in the city until further notice. The populace fragmented into opposing camps, and in their confrontation the civil and religious authorities were supported by one group or the other. But after six months of siege the Clarissans were still alive and on a war footing, until the discovery of a secret tunnel used by their partisans to supply them with food. The Franciscans, this time with the backing of a new governor, violated the cloistered recesses of Santa Clara and drove out the nuns.

It took twenty years for tempers to cool and the dismantled convent to be restored to the Clarissans, but after a century Josefa Miranda was still simmering in rancor. She inculcated the novices with her animosity, nurtured it in her will rather than her heart and embodied all responsibility for its existence in Bishop de Cáceres y Virtudes and everything in any way related to him. Her reaction, therefore, was predictable when she was told that the Marquis de Casalduero, by order of the Bishop, had brought his twelve-year-old daughter, who showed mortal symptoms of demonic possession, to the convent. She asked only one question: 'But does any such marquis exist?' Her query was doubly venomous, because the affair had to do with the Bishop and because she had always denied the legitimacy of American-born aristocrats, whom she called 'gutter nobility'.

It was time for the midday meal, and she had not been able to find Sierva María in the convent. The gatekeeper had told one of the vicars that at dawn a man in mourning had handed over a fair-haired girl dressed like a queen, but she had learned nothing more about her because just at that moment the beggars were fighting over the Palm Sunday cassava soup. To prove her veracity she gave the vicar the hat with colored ribbons. The vicar showed it to the Abbess when they were looking for the girl, and the Abbess had no doubt regarding the owner. She picked it up with her fingertips and observed it at arm's length.

'A real little marquise with the hat of a slut,' she said. 'Satan knows what he is doing.'

On her way to the locutory at nine that morning the Abbess had passed through the garden and spent some time there discussing the cost of work on the water-pipes with the masons, but she did not see the girl sitting on the stone bench. Other nuns who had walked through the garden at various times did not see her either. The two novices who took her ring swore they did not see her when they passed by the bench after the singing of Terce.

The Abbess had just awakened from her siesta when she heard a melody sung by a voice that filled the entire convent. She pulled the cord that hung beside her bed, and a novice appeared at once in the darkened room. The Abbess asked who was singing with so much skill.

'The girl,' said the novice.

Still half asleep, the Abbess murmured, 'What a beautiful voice.' And then she sat up with a start. 'What girl?'

'I don't know,' said the novice. 'The one who's had the back courtyard in an uproar since this morning.'

'By the Blessed Sacrament!' shouted the Abbess.

She leapt from her bed. Guided by the voice, she raced through the convent to the slaves' courtyard. Sierva María, with her hair spread out along the ground, sat on a stool and sang, surrounded by enchanted servants. When she saw the Abbess she stopped singing. The Abbess raised the crucifix she wore around her neck.

'Hail Mary Most Pure,' she said.

'Conceived without sin,' they all said.

The Abbess brandished the crucifix as if it were a weapon against Sierva María. '*Vade retro*,' she shouted. The slaves retreated and left the girl isolated in her space, eyes fixed and on her guard.

'Spawn of Satan!' shouted the Abbess. 'You became invisible to confound us.'

They could not make her say a word. A novice tried to lead Sierva María away by the hand, but the terrified Abbess stopped her. 'Do not touch her!' she shouted. And then to everyone, 'No one is to touch her.'

In the end they took her by force, kicking and snapping at the air like a dog, to the farthest cell in the prison pavilion. On the way they realized she was soiled with her own excrement and washed her down with buckets of water at the stable.

'So many convents in this city, and His Grace the Bishop sends us turds,' the Abbess protested.

The cell was large, with rough walls and a high ceiling that had termite tracks in the coffers. Next to the only door was a full-length window, its stout bars made of lathed wood and its frame secured by an iron crosspiece.

On the far wall, facing the sea, a high window was sealed by a wooden lattice. The bed was a concrete base covered by a canvas mattress filled with straw and stained with use. A built-in stone bench and a work table that also served as an altar and washstand were beneath a solitary crucifix nailed into the wall. They left Sierva María there, drenched all the way to her braid and trembling with fear, in the care of a warder trained in winning the millenarian war against the demon.

Sierva María sat down on the narrow bed, looking at the iron bars on the reinforced door, and this is how the servant found her when she brought a supper tray at five o'clock. The girl did not stir. The servant tried to remove her necklaces, and Sierva María seized her by the wrist and forced her to let them go. In the acta of the convent which began to be recorded that night, the servant declared that a supernatural force had thrown her to the ground.

The girl sat motionless while the door was closed, and the chain rattled and two turns of the key sounded in the lock. She looked at the food: a few shreds of dried meat, a piece of cassava bread and a cup of chocolate. She bit into the cassava bread, chewed it, spat it out. She lay down on her back. She heard the gasp of the sea, the wind heavy with rain, the first thunder of the season approaching. At dawn the next day, when the servant returned with breakfast, she found the girl sleeping on the straw stuffing of the mattress she had disemboweled with her teeth and nails.

At midday she allowed herself to be led to the refectory for those who had not yet taken their reclusive vows. It was a spacious room with a high vaulted ceiling and large windows through which the brilliance of the sea came clamoring in and the uproar at the cliffs sounded very close. Twenty novices, most of them young, were sitting at a double row of long, rough tables. They wore ordinary serge habits, their heads were shaved and they were cheerful and silly and did not hide the excitement of eating their barracks rations at the same table as one possessed. Sierva María sat near the main door, between two distracted warders, and ate almost nothing. They had dressed her in a gown like the ones worn by the novices and in her slippers, which were still damp. No one looked at her while they ate, but when the meal was over, several novices gathered around to admire her beads. One tried to take them off. Sierva María went into a rage. She shoved away the warders, who attempted to subdue her, climbed onto the table, and ran from one end to the other in a rampage of destruction, shrieking as if truly possessed. She broke everything in her path, then leapt through the window and wrecked the arbors in the courtyard, upset the beehives and knocked over the railings in the stables and the fences around the corrals. The bees flew away, and the animals, bellowing with panic, stampeded as far as the cloistered sleeping quarters.

From then on, nothing occurred that was not attributed to the pernicious influence of Sierva María. Several novices declared in the acta that she flew on transparent wings that emitted a strange humming. Two days and a squadron of slaves were needed to round up the livestock and shepherd the bees back to their honeycombs and put the house in order. Rumors circulated to the effect that the pigs had been poisoned, that the water induced prophetic visions, that one of the frightened hens flew above the rooftops and out to sea, disappearing over the horizon. But the terrors of the Clarissans were inconsistent, for despite the emotional displays of the Abbess and the dread that each of them felt, Sierva María's cell became the focus of everyone's curiosity.

Curfew in the cloister was in effect from the singing of Vespers at seven in the evening until the hour of Prime and six-o'clock Mass. All lights were extinguished except for those in a few authorized cells. Yet never before had life in the convent been so agitated and free. There was a traffic of shadows along the corridors, of intermittent whispers and haste held in check. They gambled in the most unexpected cells, either with Spanish decks of cards or weighted dice and drank furtive liquors and smoked the tobacco rolled in secret ever since Josefa Miranda had forbidden it in the cloister. The presence inside the convent walls of a girl possessed by demons had all the excitement of an extraordinary adventure.

Even the most rigid nuns slipped out of the cloister after curfew and went in groups of two or three to talk to Sierva María. She greeted them with her nails but soon learned to deal with them according to each one's personality and each night's mood. A frequent request was that she serve as their intermediary with the devil to ask for impossible favors. Sierva María would imitate voices from beyond the grave, voices of those who had been decapitated, voices of the spawn of Satan, and many believed her sly deceptions and attested to their truth in the acta. A band of nuns in disguise attacked the cell one evil night, gagged Sierva María and stripped her of the sacred necklaces. It was an ephemeral victory. As they hurried away, the commander of the raiding party stumbled and fell on the dark stairs and fractured her skull. Her companions did not have a moment's peace until they returned the stolen necklaces to their owner. No one disturbed the nights in her cell again.

For the Marquis de Casalduero, these were days of mourning. It had taken him longer to confine the girl than to repent of his action and he suffered an attack of melancholy from which he never recovered. He spent several hours prowling around the convent, wondering at which of the countless windows Sierva María was thinking of him. When he returned home, he saw Bernarda in the courtyard enjoying the cool air of early evening. He was shaken by a premonition that she would ask about Sierva María, but she did not even look at him.

He let the mastiffs out of their cages and lay down in the hammock in his bedroom, hoping to sleep forever. But he could not. The trade winds had passed, and the night was burning. The swamps sent out all kinds of insects dazed by the sweltering heat, along with clouds of carnivorous mosquitoes, and it was necessary to burn cattle dung in the bedrooms to drive them away. Souls sank into lethargy. This was the time of year when the first rainstorm was hoped for with as much longing as that with which perpetual clear weather would be prayed for six months later.

At daybreak the Marquis went to Abrenuncio's house. He had just sat down when he felt in advance the immense relief of sharing his sorrow. He came to the point with no preambles: 'I have left the girl in Santa Clara.'

Abrenuncio did not understand, and the Marquis took advantage of his confusion to deliver the next blow.

'She is to be exorcised,' he said.

The physician gave a deep sigh and said with exemplary calm, 'Tell me everything.'

Then the Marquis told him about his visit to the Bishop, his desire to pray, his blind decision, his sleepless night. It was the confession of an Old Christian who did not hold back a single secret for his own enjoyment.

'I am convinced it was a commandment from God,' he concluded.

'You mean you have recovered your faith,' said Abrenuncio.

'One never quite stops believing,' said the Marquis. 'Some doubt remains forever.'

Abrenuncio understood. He had always thought that ceasing to believe caused a permanent scar in the place where one's faith had been, making it impossible to forget. What did seem inconceivable to him was subjecting one's child to the castigation of exorcism.

'There is not much difference between that and the witchcraft of the blacks,' he said. 'In fact, it is even worse, because the blacks only sacrifice roosters to their gods, while the Holy Office is happy to break innocents on the rack or burn them alive in a public spectacle.'

The presence of Monsignor Cayetano Delaura during the Marquis's visit with the Bishop seemed a sinister precedent. 'He is an executioner,' Abrenuncio said with no elaboration. And then he became involved in an erudite listing of ancient autos-da-fé carried out against mental patients who had been executed for demonic possession or heresy.

'I think that killing her would have been more Christian than burying her alive,' he concluded.

The Marquis crossed himself. Abrenuncio looked at him, tremulous and phantasmal in his mourning taffetas and again saw in his eyes the fireflies of uncertainty that had been with him since birth.

'Take her out of there,' he said.

'It is what I have wanted to do since I saw her walking toward the pavilion of those interred in life,' said the Marquis. 'But I do not feel as if I have the strength to oppose the will of God.'

'Well, start to feel as if you did,' said Abrenuncio. 'Perhaps God will thank you some day.'

That night the Marquis requested an audience with the Bishop. He wrote the letter himself, in a circuitous style and a childish hand, and gave it to the porter in person to be sure it would reach its destination.

The Bishop was informed on Monday that Sierva María was ready for exorcism. He had finished his afternoon meal on the terrace with yellow bellflowers and took no special notice of the message. He ate little, but with a circumspection that could prolong the ritual for three hours. Sitting across from him, Father Cayetano Delaura was reading aloud in a measured voice and somewhat theatrical style. Both qualities suited the books that he chose according to his own taste and judgment.

The old palace was too large for the Bishop, for whom the reception room and bedroom and the open terrace where he took his siestas and meals until the rains began were sufficient. In the opposite wing was the official library, founded, enriched and sustained with a master hand by Cayetano Delaura, and in its time considered one of the best in the Indies. The rest of the building consisted of eleven closed chambers where the debris of two centuries had accumulated.

Except for the nun who served his food, Cayetano Delaura was the only person with access to the Bishop's house during meals, not because of personal privilege, as some said, but because of his position as reader. He did not have a definite office or any title other than librarian, but he was considered a *de facto* vicar because of his close association with the Bishop, and no one could imagine the prelate making an important decision without him. He had his own cell in an adjoining house that had interior passageways to the palace and contained the offices and living quarters of diocesan officials and the half-dozen nuns in the Bishop's domestic service. His true home, however, was the library, where he spent as many as fourteen hours a day working and reading, and where he kept a campaign cot for the times he was caught off guard by sleep.

The surprise on this historic afternoon was that Delaura had faltered several times in his reading. And even more unusual was that he skipped a page without realizing it and went on reading. The Bishop observed him through his tiny alchemist's spectacles until he turned the page. Then he interrupted, amused, 'What are you thinking about?'

Delaura gave a start.

'It must be the heat,' he said. 'Why?'

The Bishop continued to look into his eyes. 'I am sure it is something more than the heat,' he said. And in the same tone he repeated, 'What were you thinking about?'

'The girl,' said Delaura.

He was not more specific, for ever since the visit of the

Marquis there had been no other girl in the world as far as they were concerned. They had discussed her at length. Together they had reviewed histories of possession and the chronicles of saints who had performed exorcisms. Delaura sighed, 'I dreamed about her.'

'How could you dream about a person you have never seen?' asked the Bishop.

'She was a little twelve-year-old American-born marquise with hair that trailed after her like a queen's mantle,' he said. 'How could it be anyone else?'

The Bishop was not a man given to celestial visions, or miracles, or flagellations. His kingdom was of this world. And so he nodded without conviction and continued to eat. Delaura resumed reading with more care. The Bishop finished his meal, and Delaura helped him sit down in his rocking chair. When he was settled and comfortable, the Bishop said, 'And now, tell me the dream.'

It was very simple. Delaura had dreamed that Sierva María sat at a window overlooking a snow-covered field, eating grapes one by one from a cluster she held in her lap. Each grape she pulled off grew back again on the cluster. In the dream it was evident the girl had spent many years at that infinite window trying to finish the cluster, and was in no hurry to do so because she knew that in the last grape lay death.

'The strangest part,' concluded Delaura, 'is that the window through which she looked at the field was the one in Salamanca, during that winter when it snowed for three days and the lambs suffocated in the snow.'

The Bishop was moved. He knew and loved Cayetano Delaura too well to ignore the enigmas of his dreams. He had earned the place he occupied, in the diocese and in his affections, through his many talents and good character. The Bishop closed his eyes to sleep the three minutes of his late-afternoon siesta.

In the meantime, Delaura ate at the same table before they said evening prayers together. He was still eating when the Bishop stirred in the rocking chair and made the decision of his life: 'You take charge of the case.'

He spoke without opening his eyes and emitted a lion's snore. Delaura finished his meal and sat down in his usual armchair beneath the flowering vines. Then the Bishop opened his eyes.

'You have not answered me,' he said.

'I thought you were talking in your sleep,' said Delaura.

'Now I am saying it again, when I am awake,' said the Bishop. 'I entrust the girl's health to you.'

'This is the strangest thing that has ever happened to me,' said Delaura.

'Do you mean you refuse?'

'I am not an exorcist, Father,' said Delaura. 'I do not have the character or the training or the knowledge to claim to be one. Besides, we know that God has set me on another path.'

It was true. Because of certain measures taken by the Bishop, Delaura was one of three candidates for the position of Curator of the Sephardic collection at the Vatican Library. But this was the first time it had been mentioned between them, although they both knew it.

'That is even more reason,' said the Bishop. 'The girl's case, brought to a successful conclusion, may be the impetus we need.'

Delaura was aware of his own awkwardness with women. To him they seemed endowed with an untransferable use of reason that allowed them to navigate without difficulty among the hazards of reality. The mere idea of an encounter, even with a defenseless child like Sierva María, turned the perspiration on his palms to ice.

'No, Señor,' he decided. 'I do not feel qualified.'

'You not only are,' replied the Bishop, 'but you have more than enough of what someone else would be lacking: inspiration.'

It was too great a word not to be the last. The Bishop, however, did not insist on his immediate acceptance, but granted him a period of reflection, until after the penance of Holy Week, which began that day.

'Go to see the girl,' he said. 'Make a thorough study of the case, and report back to me.'

This was how Cayetano Alcino del Espíritu Santo Delaura y Escudero, at the age of thirty-six, entered the life of Sierva María and the history of the city. He had been the Bishop's student when he held the celebrated chair of theology at Salamanca, where Delaura had graduated with highest honors. He was convinced that his father was a direct descendant of Garcilaso de la Vega, whom he held in almost religious reverence, and he did not hesitate to make this known. His mother was from San Martín de Loba in the province of Mompox and had emigrated to Spain with her parents. Delaura had not believed he resembled her in any way until he reached the New Kingdom of Granada and recognized his hereditary nostalgia.

From his first conversation with Delaura in Salamanca, Bishop de Cáceres y Virtudes had felt he was in the presence of one of those rare figures who adorned the

Christianity of his time. It was a frozen February morning, and through the window one could see the snow-covered fields and, in the distance, the row of poplars along the river. The wintry landscape would be the frame of a recurrent dream that was to pursue the young theologian for the rest of his life.

They talked of books, of course, and the Bishop could not believe that Delaura had read so much at his age. He spoke to the Bishop about Garcilaso. His mentor confessed he did not know him very well but remembered him as a pagan poet who had not mentioned God more than twice in all his work.

'More times than that,' said Delaura. 'But during the Renaissance this was not unusual, even among good Catholics.'

On the day Delaura took his first vows, his mentor proposed that he accompany him to the uncertain kingdom of Yucatán, where he had just been named bishop. For Delaura, who knew life through books, the vast world of his mother seemed a dream that would never be his. While petrified lambs were being dug out of the snow, he had difficulty imagining the oppressive heat, the eternal stink of carrion, the steaming swamps. For the Bishop, who had fought in the African wars, it was easier to conceive of them.

'I have heard that our clerics go mad with joy in the Indies,' said Delaura.

'And some hang themselves,' said the Bishop. 'It is a kingdom menaced by sodomy, idolatry and anthropophagy.' And he added without bias: 'Like the land of the Moors.'

But he also thought that this was its greatest attraction.

There was a need for warriors as capable of imposing the gifts of Christian civilization as of preaching in the desert. At the age of twenty-three, however, Delaura believed that his road to the right hand of the Holy Spirit, toward whom he felt absolute devotion, had already been decided.

'All my life I have dreamed of being a chief librarian,' he said. 'It is the only work I am fit for.'

He had taken part in the public examinations for a position in Toledo that would be the first step toward realizing his dream and he was certain he would receive the appointment. But his mentor was obstinate.

'It is easier to become a saint as a librarian in Yucatán than as a martyr in Toledo,' he said.

Delaura replied with no humility, 'If God is willing, I would rather be an angel than a saint.'

He was still thinking over his mentor's offer when he was named to the post in Toledo, but he chose Yucatán instead. Delaura and the Bishop never arrived, however. They were shipwrecked in the Windward Passage after seventy days of rough seas and were rescued by a battered convoy that abandoned them to their fate at Santa María la Antigua in Darien. They spent more than a year there, waiting for the illusory mails carried by the Galleon Fleet, until de Cáceres was named interim bishop of these lands, whose see was left vacant at the sudden death of the titular bishop. When he saw the colossal jungle of Urabá from the small vessel carrying them to their new destination, Delaura recognized the nostalgia that had tormented his mother during the lugubrious winters of Toledo. The hallucinatory twilights, the nightmarish birds, the exquisite putrefactions of the mangrove swamps, seemed the cherished memories of a past he had not lived.

'Only the Holy Spirit could have arranged things so well and brought me to the land of my mother,' he said.

Twelve years later the Bishop had renounced the dream of Yucatán. He had lived a full seventy-three years, he was dying of asthma and he knew he would never again watch the snow fall in Salamanca. At the time Sierva María entered the convent, he had decided to retire once he had smoothed the road to Rome for his disciple.

The next day Cayetano Delaura went to the Convent of Santa Clara. Despite the heat he wore a habit of raw wool and carried a flask of holy water and a casket with sacramental oils, primary weapons in the war against the demon. The Abbess had never seen him, but talk of his intelligence and power had penetrated the silence of the cloister. When she received him in the locutory at six in the morning, she was struck by his air of youth, his pallor worthy of a martyr, the timbre of his voice, the enigma of his lock of white hair. But no virtue would have been enough to make her forget that he was the soldier of the Bishop. All that Delaura noticed, though, was the uproarious crowing of the roosters.

'There are only six of them, but they make enough noise for a hundred,' said the Abbess. 'Furthermore, a pig spoke and a goat gave birth to triplets.' And she added with fervor, 'Everything has been like this since your Bishop did us the favor of sending us his poisoned gift.'

She viewed with equal alarm the garden flowering with so much vigor that it seemed *contra natura*. As they walked across it she pointed out to Delaura that there were flowers of exceptional size and color, some with an unbearable scent. As far as she was concerned, everything ordinary had something supernatural about it. With each word Delaura felt that she was stronger than he, and he hastened to sharpen his weapons.

'We have not stated that the girl is possessed,' he said, 'but only that there are reasons to suspect it.'

'What we are witnessing speaks for itself,' said the Abbess.

'Take care,' said Delaura. 'Sometimes we attribute certain things we do not understand to the demon, not thinking they may be things of God that we do not understand.'

'Saint Thomas said it, and I will be guided by him,' said the Abbess: '"One must not believe demons even when they speak the truth."'

The cloistered silence began on the second floor. On one side were the empty cells, locked and bolted during the day, and facing them was a row of windows opened to the splendor of the sea. The novices did not seem to be distracted from their labors, but in reality they followed every move of the Abbess and her visitor as they made their way toward the prison pavilion.

Before they came to the far end of the corridor, where Sierva María was confined, they passed the cell of Martina Laborde, a former nun condemned to life imprisonment for having murdered two of her companions with a carving knife. She never confessed her motive. She had spent eleven years there and was better known for her failed escape attempts than for her crime. She never accepted that being imprisoned for life was the same as being a cloistered nun, and in this she was so consistent that she had offered to serve the rest of her sentence as a maid in the pavilion of those interred in life. Her implacable obsession, to which she devoted the same zeal she brought to her faith, was to be free even if she had to kill again.

Delaura could not resist his rather puerile curiosity and peered into the cell through the iron bars at the window. Martina's back was to him. When she sensed someone looking at her, she turned toward the door, and Delaura felt at once the power of her charm. An uneasy Abbess moved him away from the window.

'Take care,' she said. 'That creature is capable of anything.'

'So much a threat, even behind bars?' said Delaura.

'That much and more,' said the Abbess. 'If it were up to me, she would have been released long ago. The perturbation she causes is too great for this convent.'

When the warder opened the door, Sierva María's cell exhaled a breath of decay. The girl lay on her back on the stone bed with no mattress, her feet and hands bound with leather straps. She seemed dead, but her eyes held the light of the sea. Delaura thought she was identical to the girl in his dream, and a tremor took control of his body and soaked him in icy perspiration. He closed his eyes and prayed in a low voice, with all the weight of his faith, and when he finished he had regained his composure.

'Even if she were not possessed by any demon,' he said, 'this poor creature is in the most propitious environment for becoming so.'

The Abbess replied, 'This is an honor we do not deserve.' For they had done everything to keep the cell in the best condition, yet Sierva María generated her own dung heap.

'Our war is not against her but against the demons who may inhabit her,' said Delaura.

He entered on tiptoe to avoid the filth on the floor and sprinkled the cell with the hyssop of holy water, murmuring the ritual formulas. The Abbess was terrified by the stains the water left on the walls.

'Blood!' she screamed.

Delaura challenged the frivolity of her reasoning. Just because the water was red, that did not mean it had to be blood, and even if it were, that did not mean it had to be diabolical. 'It would be more reasonable to assume this is a miracle, and that power belongs only to God,' he said. It was neither one thing nor the other, however, for when the spots dried on the whitewashed walls, they had changed from red to an intense green. The Abbess blushed. Not only the Clarissans but all the women of her day were forbidden any kind of formal education, yet from the time she was very young she had learned scholastic argumentation in her family of distinguished theologians and great heretics.

'At least,' she replied, 'let us not deny to demons the simple power to change the color of blood.'

'Nothing is more useful than a timely doubt,' was Delaura's immediate retort, and he looked straight at her. 'Read Saint Augustine.'

'I have already read him with great care,' said the Abbess.

'Well, read him again,' said Delaura.

Before turning his attention to the girl, he asked the warder in a very courteous tone to leave the cell. Then, without the same sweetness, he told the Abbess, 'You too, please.'

'On your responsibility,' she said.

'The Bishop is the highest authority,' he said.

'There is no need to remind me of that,' said the Abbess with a touch of sarcasm. 'We know by now that you are the masters of God.'

Delaura granted her the pleasure of the last word. He sat on the edge of the bed and examined the girl with the thoroughness of a physician. He continued to tremble but no longer perspired.

Seen at close quarters, Sierva María was scratched and bruised, and her skin was chafed raw by the straps. But what affected him most was the wound on her ankle, inflamed and festering as a result of the healers' ineptitude.

As he examined her, Delaura explained that she had been brought there not to be martyrized but because of the suspicion that a demon had entered her body in order to steal her soul. He needed her help to establish the truth. But it was impossible to know whether she was listening and whether she understood that it was a plea from the heart.

When he had completed the examination, Delaura requested a chest of medicines but did not permit the apothecary nun to enter the cell. He applied balsams to the girl's wounds and with gentle breaths relieved the burning on her raw skin, astounded at her tolerance of pain. Sierva María answered none of his questions, showed no interest in his preaching and complained about nothing.

It was a discouraging start that pursued Delaura until

he reached the calm waters of the library. The largest room in the Bishop's house, it did not have a single window, and the walls were lined with glass-doored mahogany cabinets containing numerous books arranged in careful order. In the center of the room stood a large table that held maritime charts, an astrolabe and other navigational instruments, and a globe of the earth with additions and emendations that successive cartographers had made by hand as the size of the world increased. In the rear was a rustic work table with an inkwell, penknife, turkey quills for writing, sand to dry the ink and a withered carnation in a vase. The entire room was in shadow and had the odor of paper at rest and the coolness and peace of a forest glade.

In a smaller enclosure at the back of the room was a locked cabinet with doors made of ordinary lumber. This was the prison of forbidden books, purged by the Holy Inquisition because they dealt with 'deceptive and profane matters, and false histories'. No one had access to it but Cayetano Delaura, who had pontifical permission to explore the abysses of written works gone astray.

From the moment he first saw Sierva María, those calm waters of so many years became his inferno. He would not meet there again with his friends, the clergy and laymen who shared with him the delight of pure ideas and organized scholastic tourneys, literary gatherings, musical evenings. His passion was reduced to understanding the wily deceptions of the demon, and for five days and nights he devoted all his reading and reflection to the subject before he returned to the convent. On Monday, when the Bishop saw him leave with a firm step, he asked him how he felt.

'As if I had the wings of the Holy Spirit,' said Delaura.

He had put on his cassock of ordinary cotton, which filled him with the courage of a woodcutter, and his soul wore armor against despair. They stood him in good stead. The warder responded to his greeting with a grunt, Sierva María received him with an ill-tempered frown, and it was difficult to breathe in the cell because excrement and the remains of earlier meals were strewn over the floor. On the altar, next to the Sanctuary Lamp, the midday meal lay untouched. Delaura picked up the plate and offered the girl a spoonful of black beans in coagulated grease. She turned her head. He insisted several times, but her response was always the same. Then Delaura put the spoonful of beans in his mouth, tasted it, and swallowed without chewing, showing real signs of repugnance.

'You are right,' he told her. 'This is vile.'

The girl did not pay the slightest attention to him. When he treated her inflamed ankle, the skin twitched and her eyes filled with tears. He thought she had surrendered, and he comforted her with the murmurings of a good shepherd, and at last dared loosen the straps to give her ravaged body some respite. The girl flexed her fingers several times to feel whether they were still hers and stretched her feet numbed by the bindings. Then she looked at Delaura for the first time, weighed and measured him and attacked with the well-aimed pounce of a hunted animal. The warder helped subdue her and tighten the straps again. Before he left, Delaura took a sandalwood rosary from his pocket and hung it around Sierva María's neck over her Santería beads.

The Bishop was alarmed when he saw him return with

scratches on his face and a bite on his hand, the mere sight of which caused him distress. But he was even more alarmed by Delaura's reaction. He displayed his wounds as if they were battle trophies and scoffed at the danger of contracting rabies. The Bishop's physician, however, treated them with utmost seriousness, for he was one of those who feared that the eclipse on the following Monday would be the prelude to grave disasters.

On the other hand, the murderer Martina Laborde did not encounter the least resistance in Sierva María. She had tiptoed to her cell, as if by chance, and seen her in the bed, tied by her feet and hands. The girl went on the defensive and kept her eyes fixed and alert until Martina smiled. Then she smiled too, and her surrender was unconditional. It was as if the soul of Dominga de Adviento had filled the entire cell.

Martina told her who she was and why she was there for the rest of her days, even though she had grown hoarse proclaiming her innocence. When Martina asked Sierva María the reasons for her confinement, she could tell her only the little she had learned from her exorcist: 'I have a devil inside.'

Martina asked no more questions, assuming that the girl lied or had been lied to, not realizing she was one of the few white women to whom Sierva María had told the truth. She gave her a demonstration of the art of embroidery, and the girl asked to be freed so that she could try it too. Martina showed her the scissors she carried in the pocket of her gown along with other items used for needlework.

'What you want is for me to free you,' she said. 'But I

warn you: If you try to hurt me, I have the means to kill you.'

Sierva María did not doubt her determination. She was freed and she repeated the embroidery lesson with the facility and good ear with which she had learned to play the theorbo. Before Martina left, she promised to obtain permission for them to watch the total eclipse of the sun together on the following Monday.

At dawn on Friday the swallows took their leave, making a wide circle in the sky and showering the streets and rooftops with a foul-smelling indigo snowstorm. It was difficult to eat and sleep until the midday sun dried the stubborn droppings and the night breezes purified the air. But terror prevailed. No one had ever seen swallows shit in mid-flight or heard of the stink of their excrement interfering with ordinary life.

In the convent, of course, no one doubted that Sierva María had the power to change the laws of migration. On Sunday after Mass Delaura could even feel the hardness in the air as he crossed the garden with a little basket of pastries from the arcades. Sierva María, remote from everything, still wore the rosary around her neck but did not respond to his greeting or deign to look at him. He sat beside her, chewed a cruller from the basket with delight, and said, his mouth full, 'It tastes like heaven.'

He brought the other half of the cruller to Sierva María's mouth. She turned her head, not facing the wall as she had on other occasions but indicating to Delaura that the warder was spying on them. He made an emphatic gesture with his hand in the direction of the door.

'Get away from there,' he ordered.

When the warder moved away, the girl tried to satisfy her long-standing hunger with the half of the cruller, but spat out the piece she had bitten off. 'It tastes like swallow shit,' she said. Still, her humor changed. She cooperated when Delaura treated the painful raw spots on her back, and paid attention to him for the first time when she saw his bandaged hand. With an innocence that could not be feigned, she asked what had happened.

'I was bitten by a little rabid dog with a tail more than a meter long.'

Sierva María wanted to see the wound. Delaura removed the bandage, and with her index finger she touched the crimson halo of swelling as if it were a burning coal, and laughed for the first time.

'I'm worse than the plague,' she said.

Delaura responded not with the Gospels but with Garcilaso: '*Well may you do this to one who can endure it.*'

He burned with the revelation that something immense and irreparable had begun to occur in his life. When he left the warder reminded him, on behalf of the Abbess, that it was forbidden to bring in provisions from the street because of the danger the food might be poisoned, as it had been during the siege. Delaura lied and said he had brought the basket with the permission of the Bishop, and lodged a formal complaint about the bad food served to those confined in a convent famous for its fine cuisine.

During supper he read to the Bishop with renewed enthusiasm. As always, he joined him in the evening prayers, closing his eyes to make it easier to think of Sierva María as he prayed. He retired to the library earlier than usual, thinking of her, and the more he thought the stronger grew his desire to think. He recited aloud the love sonnets of Garcilaso, torn by the suspicion that every verse contained an enigmatic portent that had something to do with his life. He could not sleep. At dawn he was slumped over the desk, his forehead pressing against the book he had not read. From the depths of sleep he heard the three nocturns of the new day's Matins in the adjacent sanctuary. 'God save you, María de Todos los Ángeles,' he said in his sleep. His own voice startled him awake, and in her inmate's tunic, with her fiery hair spilling over her shoulders, he saw Sierva María discard the old carnation and place a bouquet of newly opened gardenias in the vase on his work table. Delaura, with Garcilaso, told her in an ardent voice: '*For you was I born, for you do I have life, for you will I die, for you am I now dying*.' Sierva María smiled without looking at him. He closed his eyes to be sure she was not an illusion of the shadows. When he opened them the vision had disappeared, but the library was saturated with the scent of her gardenias.

Four

Father Cayetano Delaura was invited by the Bishop to wait for the eclipse beneath the canopy of yellow bell-flowers, the only place in the house with a view of the ocean sky. The pelicans, motionless in the air on out-spread wings, seemed to have died in mid-flight. The Bishop, who had just finished his siesta, moved a slow fan in a hammock hung from naval capstans on two wooden support beams. Delaura sat beside him in a wicker rocking chair. Both were in a state of grace, drinking tamarind water and looking over the rooftops at the vast cloudless sky. Just after two it began to grow dark, the hens huddled on their perches, and all the stars came out at the same time. The world trembled in a supernatural shudder. The Bishop heard the fluttering wings of laggard doves searching for their lofts in the darkness.

'God is great,' he sighed. 'Even the animals feel it.'

The nun in his service brought a candle and several pieces of smoked glass for looking at the sun. The Bishop sat up in the hammock and began to observe the eclipse through the glass.

'You must look with only one eye,' he said, trying to control the whistle of his breathing. 'If not, you run the risk of losing both.'

Delaura held the glass in his hand but did not look at the eclipse. After a long silence, the Bishop scrutinized him in the darkness and saw his luminous eyes indifferent to the enchantment of the counterfeit night.

'What are you thinking about?' he asked.

Delaura did not reply. He looked at the sun and saw a waning moon that hurt his retina despite the dark glass. But he did not stop looking.

'You are still thinking about the girl,' said the Bishop.

Cayetano was startled, despite the fact that the Bishop made this kind of accurate guess with almost unnatural frequency. 'I was thinking that the common people will relate their troubles to this eclipse,' he said. The Bishop shook his head without looking away from the sky.

'Who knows, they may be right,' he said. 'The cards of the Lord are not easy to read.'

'This phenomenon was calculated thousands of years ago by Assyrian astronomers,' said Delaura.

'That is the answer of a Jesuit,' said the Bishop.

Cayetano continued to observe the sun, not using the glass out of simple distraction. At twelve minutes past two the sun looked like a perfect black disc, and for an instant it was midnight in the middle of the day. Then the eclipse recovered its earthbound quality, and dawn's roosters began to crow. When Delaura stopped looking, the medal of fire persisted on his retina.

'I still see the eclipse,' he said, amused. 'Wherever I look it is there.'

The Bishop considered the spectacle finished. 'It will go away in a few hours,' he said. He stretched and yawned as he sat in the hammock and gave thanks to God for the new day.

Delaura had not lost the thread of their conversation.

'With all due respect, Father,' he said, 'I do not believe the child is possessed.'

This time the Bishop was alarmed in earnest.

'Why do you say that?'

'I believe she is only terrified,' said Delaura.

'We have an abundance of proof,' said the Bishop. 'Or have you not read the acta?'

Yes. Delaura had studied them with great care, and they were more useful for understanding the mentality of the Abbess than the condition of Sierva María. They had exorcised the places where the girl had been on the morning she entered the convent, as well as everything she had touched. Those who had been in contact with her had submitted to fasting and purification. The novice who had stolen her ring on the first day was condemned to forced labor in the garden. They said the girl had enjoyed quartering a goat whose throat she slit with her own hands and had eaten its testicles and eyes with spices as hot as fire. She had displayed a gift for languages that allowed her to talk with Africans from any nation better than they could among themselves, or with any sort of animal. The day after her arrival, the eleven captive macaws that had adorned the garden for twenty years died for no apparent reason. She had charmed the servants with demonic songs sung in voices other than her own. When she learned that the Abbess was looking for her, she had made herself invisible only to her eyes.

'I believe, however,' said Delaura, 'that what seems demonic to us are the customs of the blacks, learned by the girl as a consequence of the neglected condition in which her parents kept her.'

'Take care!' the Bishop warned. 'The Enemy makes better use of our intelligence than of our errors.'

'Then the best gift we could give him would be to exorcise a healthy child,' said Delaura.

The Bishop bristled. 'Ought I to assume that you are in a state of defiance?'

'You ought to assume that I have my doubts, Father,' said Delaura. 'But I obey in all humility.'

And so he returned to the convent without having convinced the Bishop. Over his left eye he wore the patch that the doctor had prescribed until the sun imprinted on his retina was erased. He sensed the glances following him through the garden and along the series of corridors that led to the prison pavilion, but no one said a word to him. The entire convent seemed to be convalescing from the eclipse.

When the warder opened Sierva María's cell, Delaura felt his heart bursting in his chest, and it was all he could do to remain standing. To test her mood that morning, he asked the girl whether she had seen the eclipse. She had, in fact, from the terrace. She did not understand why he had to wear a patch over his eye, when she had looked at the sun without protection and felt fine. She told him that the nuns had watched on their knees and that the convent had been paralyzed until the roosters crowed. But to her it had not seemed anything otherworldly.

'What I saw is what I see every night,' she said.

Something had changed in her that Delaura could not define, and its most visible symptom was a trace of sadness. He was not mistaken. As he began to treat her wounds, the girl stared at him with troubled eyes and said in a tremulous voice, 'I'm going to die.'

Delaura shuddered.

'Who told you that?'

'Martina,' said the girl.

'Have you seen her?'

She told him that Martina had come to her cell twice to teach her embroidery and that they had looked at the eclipse together. She said that Martina was good and gentle, and the Abbess had allowed her to hold the embroidery lessons on the terrace so they could watch the twilights over the sea.

'Aha,' he said without blinking. 'And did she tell you when you are going to die?'

The girl nodded, her lips closed tight to keep from crying.

'After the eclipse,' she said.

'After the eclipse could be the next hundred years,' said Delaura.

But he had to concentrate on the treatment so she would not notice the lump in his throat. Sierva María said no more. He looked at her again, intrigued by her silence, and saw that her eyes were wet.

'I'm afraid,' she said.

She collapsed on the bed and burst into heartrending tears. He moved closer and comforted her with the palliatives of a confessor. This was when Sierva María learned that Cayetano was her exorcist and not her physician.

'Then why are you healing me?' she asked.

His voice trembled.

'Because I love you very much.'

She was not aware of his audacity.

When he left Sierva María, Delaura stopped at Martina's cell. Close to her for the first time, he saw that she had pockmarked skin, a shorn head, a nose that was too large and the teeth of a rat, but her seductive power was a material current that could be felt at once. Delaura chose to speak to her from the doorway.

'That poor child already has enough reasons to be frightened,' he said. 'I beg you not to add to them.'

Martina was taken aback. She would never dream of predicting the day of anyone's death, least of all that of a girl who was so appealing and defenseless. She had only asked about her circumstances, and had realized after three or four answers that she lied out of habit. Martina spoke with so much gravity that Delaura knew Sierva María had lied to him as well. He asked her to forgive his rashness, and begged her to demand no explanations from the girl.

'I will know what to do,' he concluded.

Martina enveloped him in her charm. 'I know who Your Reverence is,' she said, 'and I know you have always known very well what to do.' But Delaura was wounded by this evidence that Sierva María needed no help from anyone to nurture a horror of death in the solitude of her cell.

In the course of that week Mother Josefa Miranda sent the Bishop a formal memorandum of complaints and protests written in her own hand. She asked that the Clarissans be relieved of the guardianship of Sierva María, which she considered a belated punishment for faults that had already been purged many times over. She enumerated a new list of extraordinary occurrences that had been cited in the acta and could be explained only as the consequences of shameless complicity between the girl and the demon. She ended with a furious denunciation of Cayetano Delaura's arrogance, his freethinking, his personal animosity toward her and the abusiveness of his bringing food into the convent in defiance of the prohibitions of their rule.

The Bishop showed him the memorandum as soon as he returned, and Delaura read it where he stood, not moving a muscle of his face. When he finished he was in a rage.

'If anyone is possessed by all the demons, it is Josefa Miranda,' he said. 'Demons of rancor, intolerance, imbecility. She is detestable!'

The Bishop was surprised by his vehemence. Delaura observed this and tried to speak in a calmer tone.

'What I mean,' he said, 'is that she attributes so much power to the forces of evil that she seems like a worshipper of the demon.'

'My investiture does not permit me to agree with you,' said the Bishop. 'But I would like to.'

He reprimanded Delaura for any excess he might have committed, and asked for his patience in enduring the Abbess's unfortunate nature. 'The Gospels are filled with women like her, some with even worse defects,' he said. 'And yet Jesus exalted them.' The Bishop could not continue, because the thunder resounded over the house and then rolled out to sea, and a biblical downpour cut them off from the rest of the world. The Bishop lay back in the rocking chair and was shipwrecked in nostalgia.

'How far we are!' he sighed.

'From what?'

'From ourselves,' said the Bishop. 'Does it seem reasonable to you that a man should need up to a year to learn he is an orphan?' And since there was no answer, he confessed to his homesickness: 'The very idea that they have already slept tonight in Spain fills me with terror.'

'We cannot intervene in the rotation of the earth,' said Delaura.

'But we could be unaware of it so that it does not cause us grief,' said the Bishop. 'More than faith, what Galileo lacked was a heart.'

Delaura was familiar with these crises that had tormented the Bishop on nights of melancholy rain ever since old age had assailed him. All he could do was distract him from the attack of black bile until sleep overcame him.

Toward the end of the month, a proclamation announced the imminent arrival of the new viceroy, Don Rodrigo de Buen Lozano, who would stop here for a visit on his way to the seat of government in Santa Fe de Bogotá. He was traveling with his entourage of magistrates and functionaries, servants and personal physicians, and a string quartet presented to him by the Queen to help him endure the tedium of the Indies. The Vicereine, a distant relative of the Abbess, had asked to be lodged at the convent.

Sierva María was forgotten in the heating quicklime and steaming pitch, the plague of hammering and the shouted blasphemies of all kinds of people who invaded the house as far as the cloister. A scaffolding collapsed with a deafening crash, killing a bricklayer and injuring seven other workers. The Abbess attributed the disaster to the malevolent spells of Sierva María and took advantage of this new opportunity to insist that she be sent to another convent until the festivities were concluded. This time her principal argument was the inadvisability of allowing someone possessed to be in close proximity to the Vicereine. The Bishop did not respond.

Don Rodrigo de Buen Lozano was a mature, elegant Asturian, a champion at pelota and partridge shooting, who compensated with his other attractions for being twenty-two years older than his wife. He laughed, even at himself, with his entire body, which he lost no opportunity to display. From the moment he felt the first Caribbean breezes intermingled with nocturnal drums and the fragrance of ripe guava, he removed his springtime attire and wandered bare-chested among the gatherings of ladies on board ship. He disembarked in shirtsleeves, with no speeches and no salutes by the Lombard cannon. In his honor, fandangos, *bundes* and *cumbiambas* were authorized although they had been prohibited by the Bishop, and bullfights and cockfights were held outdoors.

The Vicereine, an active and somewhat mischievous girl just past adolescence, burst into the convent like a windstorm of change. There was no corner she did not examine, no problem she did not consider, nothing good she did not wish to improve. She wandered through the convent, wanting to see everything with all the eagerness of a young novice. The Abbess, in fact, thought it prudent to spare her the unpleasant impression of the prison.

'It is not worth the visit,' she said. 'There are only two inmates, and one is possessed by the demon.'

That was enough to awaken the Vicereine's interest. She did not care at all that the cells had not been prepared and the inmates had not been notified. As soon as her door was opened, Martina Laborde threw herself at the Vicereine's feet, begging for a pardon.

It did not seem probable, after one failed escape and

another that had succeeded. She had attempted the first six years earlier, along the terrace overlooking the sea, in the company of three other nuns condemned for diverse reasons to a variety of sentences. One of them escaped. This was when the windows were sealed and the courtyard beneath the terrace was fortified. The following year, the three remaining prisoners tied up the warder, who at that time slept in the pavilion, and fled through a service door. Martina's family followed the advice of their confessor and returned her to the convent. For four long years she had been the only prisoner, with no right to receive visits in the locutory or hear Sunday Mass in the chapel. A pardon seemed impossible. The Vicereine, however, promised to intercede with her husband.

In Sierva María's cell the air was still harsh with quicklime and lingering traces of pitch, but a new order prevailed. As soon as the warder opened the door, the Vicereine felt bewitched by a glacial breath of wind. In a corner illuminated by its own light, Sierva María sat in her torn tunic and stained slippers, plying a slow needle. She did not look up until the Vicereine greeted her. In the girl's eyes she saw the irresistible force of a revelation. 'By the Blessed Sacrament,' she murmured, and stepped into the cell.

'Take care,' the Abbess whispered in her ear. 'She is like a tiger.'

The Abbess seized her arm. The Vicereine did not go in, but one glimpse of Sierva María was enough for her to resolve to save the girl.

The governor of the city, an effeminate bachelor, gave a luncheon, for men only, in honor of the Viceroy. The string quartet from Spain and a bagpipe-and-drum ensemble from San Jacinto played, and blacks in costume performed bold parodies of white dances. As a finale, a curtain at the back of the room was raised to reveal the Abyssinian slave purchased by the Governor for her weight in gold. She wore an almost transparent tunic that heightened the peril of her nakedness. After showing herself to the ordinary guests she stopped in front of the Viceroy, and the tunic slipped down her body to the floor.

Her perfection was alarming. Her shoulder had not been profaned by the slaver's brand, the initial of her first owner had not been burned on her back, and her entire person breathed an air of intimacy. The Viceroy turned pale, inhaled deeply and with a movement of his hand erased the unbearable vision from his memory.

'Take her away, for God's sake,' he ordered. 'I do not want to see her again for the rest of my days.'

Perhaps in retribution for the Governor's frivolity, the Vicereine presented Sierva María at the dinner the Abbess gave in her private dining room. Martina Laborde had warned them: 'Don't try to take away her necklaces and bracelets, and you'll see how well she behaves.' It was true. They dressed her in her grandmother's gown, the one she had worn when she came to the convent, they washed and combed her unbraided hair so that it trailed behind her, and the Vicereine herself led her by the hand to her husband's table. Even the Abbess was stunned by the girl's elegance, her physical brilliance, the prodigy of her hair. The Vicereine murmured in her husband's ear, 'She is possessed by the demon.'

The Viceroy refused to believe it. In Burgos he had seen a possessed woman who defecated without pause the entire night until she filled the room to overflowing. Trying to avoid a similar fate for Sierva María, he had her examined by his physicians. They confirmed that she showed no symptom of rabies and they agreed with Abrenuncio that it was improbable she would contract the disease now. But no one believed himself authorized to doubt she was possessed by the demon.

The Bishop took advantage of the festivities to reflect on the memorandum from the Abbess and on Sierva María's final disposition. For his part, Cayetano Delaura attempted the purification that precedes exorcism and shut himself away in the library with nothing to eat but cassava bread and water. He failed. He spent delirious nights and sleepless days writing unrestrained verses that were his only calmative for the raging desires of his body.

When the library was dismantled close to a century later, some of these poems were discovered in a sheaf of almost indecipherable papers. The first, and the only one legible in its entirety, was Delaura's recollection of himself at the age of twelve, sitting on his student's trunk under a light spring rain in the cobbled courtyard of the seminary at Ávila. He had just arrived from Toledo after several days on muleback, wearing an outfit of his father's that had been altered to fit him, and traveling with the trunk that was more than twice his weight because his mother had packed in it everything he might need to live with honor until the end of his novitiate. The porter helped him carry it to the middle of the courtyard and then left him to his fate in the rain.

'Take it up to the third floor,' the porter told him, 'and they'll show you where you sleep in the dormitory.'

In an instant the entire seminary appeared on the

balconies overlooking the courtyard, watching to see what Cayetano would do with the trunk, as if he were the single protagonist in a play known to everyone but him. When he realized that no one would help him, he removed as many things as he could carry and took them up the steep stairs of living rock to the third floor. The proctor showed him his place in the two rows of beds in the dormitory for novices. Cayetano put his things on the bed, went back to the courtyard and climbed the stairs four more times until he had finished. At last he took the empty trunk by the handle and dragged it up the staircase.

The teachers and students watching from the balconies did not turn to look at him as he passed each floor. But the Father Rector was waiting on the third-floor landing when he brought up the trunk and he began the applause. The others followed suit and gave him an ovation. Then Cayetano learned that he had passed with flying colors the first initiation rite of the seminary, which consisted of carrying one's trunk up to the dormitory without asking any questions or requesting help from anyone. His quick intelligence, good disposition and strong character were proclaimed as examples for the other novices.

But the memory that would make the greatest mark on him was his conversation on that first night in the office of the Rector, who had arranged to see him to discuss the only book found in his trunk, its binding torn and the title page missing, just as Cayetano had discovered it in one of his father's chests. He had read as much of the volume as he could during the nights of his journey, and he longed to know the ending. The Father Rector wanted to hear his opinion of it.

'I will know when I finish reading it,' he said.

The Rector, with a relieved smile, locked the volume away.

'You will never know,' he said. 'It is a forbidden book.'

Twenty-four years later, in the gloom of the diocesan library, he realized he had read every book that had passed through his hands, authorized or not, except this one. He shuddered with the sensation that an entire life had ended that day. Another, unpredictable life was beginning.

He had started afternoon prayers on the eighth day of his fast, when he was informed that the Bishop was waiting for him in the drawing room to receive the Viceroy. The visit was unplanned, even by the Viceroy. The inopportune idea had occurred to him during his first excursion through the city. He was obliged to contemplate the rooftops from the flowering terrace while urgent messages were sent to nearby functionaries and some order was imposed on the drawing room.

The Bishop received the Viceroy with six clerics from his own general staff. He sat Cayetano Delaura on his right and introduced him with no title other than his complete name. Before beginning the conversation, the Viceroy examined with commiserating eyes the peeling walls, the torn curtains, the cheap local furnishings, the clerics dripping with perspiration in their indigent habits. The Bishop said with injured pride, 'We are the sons of Joseph the Carpenter.' The Viceroy made a gesture of comprehension and launched into an account of his first week's impressions. He spoke of his illusory plans to increase trade with the English Antilles once the wounds of war had been healed, of the benefits of official intervention in education, of promoting arts and letters and bringing these colonial outposts into harmony with the rest of the world.

'These are times of renovation,' he said.

Once again the Bishop had confirmed the facile nature of secular power. He extended a trembling finger toward Delaura, not looking at him, and said to the Viceroy, 'Father Cayetano is the person here who keeps abreast of those innovations.'

The Viceroy followed the Bishop's finger and saw a remote expression and startled eyes that looked at him without blinking. His interest was real when he asked Delaura, 'Have you read Leibniz?'

'I have, Excellency,' said Delaura, and specified: 'In the course of my duties.'

By the end of the visit, it became evident that the Viceroy's greatest interest was the case of Sierva María. For its own sake, he explained, and for the peace of mind of the Abbess, whose suffering had moved him to pity.

'We still lack definitive proof, but the acta of the convent tell us that the poor creature is possessed by the demon,' said the Bishop. 'The Abbess knows this better than we do.'

'She thinks you have fallen into a snare of Satan,' said the Viceroy.

'Not we alone, but all of Spain,' said the Bishop. 'We have crossed the ocean sea to impose the law of Christ, and we have done so with Masses and processions and festivals for patron saints, but not in the souls of men.'

He spoke of Yucatán, where they had constructed sumptuous cathedrals to hide the pagan pyramids, not realizing that the natives came to Mass because their sanctuaries still lived beneath the silver altars. He spoke of the chaotic mixing of blood that had gone on since the conquest: Spanish blood with Indian blood, and both of these with blacks of every sort, even Mandingo Muslims, and he asked himself whether such miscegenation had a place in the Kingdom of God. Despite his obstructed breathing and his old-man's cough, he ended without conceding a pause to the Viceroy, 'What can all this be but snares of the Enemy?'

The Viceroy showed his distress.

'The disenchantment of Your Grace is of the utmost gravity,' he said.

'Do not view it in that light, Your Excellency,' the Bishop said in the most courteous manner. 'I am only attempting to clarify the strength of faith we require so that these peoples may be worthy of our sacrifice.'

The Viceroy returned to his original subject.

'To my best understanding, the misgivings of the Abbess are practical in nature,' he said. 'She thinks that perhaps other convents would be better suited to so difficult a case.'

'Well, Your Excellency should know that we chose Santa Clara without a moment's hesitation because of the fortitude, the competence and the authority of Josefa Miranda,' said the Bishop. 'And God knows we are not mistaken.'

'I will take the liberty of telling her so,' said the Viceroy.

'She knows it all too well,' said the Bishop. 'What concerns me is why she does not dare to believe it.'

As he spoke he felt the passing aura of an imminent

attack of asthma and he hastened to conclude the visit. He said he had received a formal memorandum of complaints from the Abbess, which he promised to resolve with the most fervent pastoral love as soon as his ill health allowed. The Viceroy thanked him and ended the visit with a personal courtesy. He too suffered from an obstinate asthma, and he offered his physicians to the Bishop. This did not seem fitting to the prelate.

'Everything that pertains to me is in the hands of God,' he said. 'I have reached the age at which the Virgin died.'

In contrast to their greetings, their leave-taking was slow and ceremonious. Three of the clerics, Delaura among them, accompanied the Viceroy in silence along the lugubrious corridors to the main entrance. The viceregal guard kept the beggars at bay with a wall of crossed halberds. Before climbing into his carriage, the Viceroy turned to Delaura, pointed at him with an unappealable finger, and said, 'Do not allow me to forget you.'

His words were so unexpected and enigmatic that Delaura could do no more than bow in response.

The Viceroy drove to the convent to tell the Abbess the outcome of his visit. Some hours later, as he was about to leave, he refused to pardon Martina Laborde, despite the repeated pleas of the Vicereine, because he thought it would set a bad precedent for the many people incarcerated for lesser crimes whom he had found in other prisons.

The Bishop had closed his eyes, leaning forward in an effort to calm his whistling breath, until Delaura returned. His assistants had withdrawn on tiptoe, and the drawing room was in shadow. When the Bishop looked around, he saw vacant chairs lined against the wall and no one but Cayetano in the room. In a very low voice he asked, 'Have we ever seen so good a man?'

Delaura responded with an ambiguous gesture. The Bishop struggled into an upright position and then leaned against the arm of the chair until he could control his breathing. He wanted no supper. Delaura brought a candle to light the way to his bedroom.

'We have not behaved well with the Viceroy,' said the Bishop.

'Was there any reason to?' asked Delaura. 'One does not knock on a bishop's door unannounced.'

The Bishop did not agree, and told him so with great vigor. 'My door is the door of the Church, and he conducted himself like an old-fashioned Christian,' he said. 'The impertinence was mine, because of the illness in my chest, and I must do something to make amends.' By the time he reached his bedroom door, he had changed his tone and the topic, and he said good night to Delaura with a familiar pat on the shoulder.

'Pray for me this night,' he said. 'I fear it will be a long one.'

He did, in fact, feel as if he were dying of the asthma attack he had foreseen during the Viceroy's visit. Since an emetic of tartar and other extreme palliatives gave him no relief, he had to undergo an emergency bleeding. By dawn he had recovered his indomitability.

Cayetano, sleepless in the nearby library, was not aware of any of this. He had just begun morning prayers when he was informed that the Bishop was waiting for him in his bedroom. The Bishop sat in bed, having a cup of chocolate with bread and cheese, and breathing like a new bellows, his spirit exalted. One glance was enough for Cayetano to know that he had reached his decisions.

It was true. Despite the request from the Abbess, Sierva María would remain at Santa Clara, and Father Cayetano Delaura, with the full confidence of the Bishop, would continue to be in charge of her case. She would no longer be kept under a prison regime and henceforth was to share in the general benefits accorded the residents of the convent. The Bishop was grateful for the acta, but their lack of rigor interfered with the clarity of the process, and therefore the exorcist was to proceed according to his own judgment. He finished by ordering Delaura to visit the Marquis on his behalf, with authority to resolve whatever might be needed until the Bishop had both the opportunity and the health to grant him an audience.

'There will be no further instructions,' were his closing words. 'May God bless you.'

Cayetano raced to the convent, his heart pounding, but did not find Sierva María in her cell. She was in the formal reception room, covered in precious gems and with her hair spilling down to her feet, posing with the exquisite dignity of a black woman for a celebrated portrait painter from the Viceroy's entourage. The intelligence with which she obeyed the artist was as admirable as her beauty. Cayetano fell into ecstasy. Sitting in the shadows and seeing her without being seen, he had more than enough time to erase any doubt from his heart.

At the hour of Nones the portrait was finished. The painter scrutinized it at a distance, gave it two or three final brushstrokes and, before signing it, asked Sierva María to look at the picture. It was a perfect likeness of her as she stood on a cloud surrounded by a court of submissive demons. She contemplated the canvas for some time and recognized herself in the splendor of her years. At last she said, 'It's like a mirror.'

'Even the demons?' asked the painter.

'That's just how they look,' she said.

The sitting was over, and Cayetano accompanied Sierva María to the cell. He had never seen her take a step, and her walk had the same ease and grace as her dancing. He had never seen her in any clothes but an inmate's cassock, and the regal gown gave her a maturity and elegance that revealed how much of a woman she had already become. They had never walked side by side, and he was charmed by the candor of their being together.

The cell was changed, thanks to the persuasive talents of the Viceroy and Vicereine, who on their farewell visit had convinced the Abbess that the Bishop's reasoning was sound. The mattress was new, there were linen sheets and down pillows, and the articles needed for daily grooming and bathing had been provided. The light of the sea poured in through the unlatticed window and sparkled on the fresh whitewash of the walls. Now that Sierva María's meals were the same as those served in the cloister, it was no longer necessary to bring her anything from the outside, but Delaura always arranged to smuggle in delicacies from the arcades.

She wanted to share her food, and Delaura accepted one of the little cakes that upheld the prestige of the Clarissans. As they ate, she remarked in passing: 'I've seen snow.'

Cayetano was not alarmed. There were tales of a viceroy long before who wanted to bring snow from the

Pyrenees to show to the natives, for he did not know we had it right next to the sea, in the Sierra Nevada de Santa Marta. Perhaps, with his innovative arts, Don Rodrigo de Buen Lozano had accomplished the feat.

'No,' said the girl. 'It was in a dream.'

She told him about it: she was sitting in front of a window where heavy snow was falling, while one by one she ate the grapes from a cluster she held in her lap. Delaura felt a brush of dread. Trembling at the imminence of a final answer, he dared to ask: 'How did it end?'

'I'm afraid to tell you,' said Sierva María.

He did not need to hear more. He closed his eyes and prayed for her. When he finished, he was a changed man.

'Don't worry,' he said. 'I promise you will soon be free and happy through the grace of the Holy Spirit.'

Bernarda had not known until then that Sierva María was in the convent. She found out almost by accident one night when she saw Dulce Olivia sweeping and straightening the house and thought she was one of her hallucinations. In search of some rational explanation, she inspected the house room by room and in the process realized she had not seen Sierva María for some time. Caridad del Cobre told her the little she knew: 'The Señor Marquis told us she was going very far away and we wouldn't see her again.' A light was burning in her husband's bedroom, and Bernarda walked in without knocking.

He lay awake in the hammock, surrounded by smoke from the cow dung burning over a slow fire to drive away mosquitoes. He saw the strange woman transfigured by her silk robe, and he too thought he was seeing an apparition, for she looked pale and faded and seemed to come from a great distance. Bernarda asked about Sierva María.

'She has not been with us for days,' he said.

She understood this in the worst possible sense and had to sit down on the closest chair to catch her breath.

'You mean that Abrenuncio did what had to be done,' she said.

The Marquis crossed himself.

'God forbid!'

He told her the truth. He was careful to explain that he had not informed her at the time because, in accordance with her wishes, he wanted to treat her as if she had died. Bernarda listened, not blinking, with more attention than she had granted him in the twelve years of their unfortunate life in common.

'I knew it would cost me my life,' said the Marquis, 'but in exchange for hers.'

Bernarda sighed. 'You mean that now our shame is public knowledge.' She saw the glimmer of a tear on her husband's eyelids, and a tremor rose from her belly. This time it was not death but the ineluctable certainty of what was bound to happen sooner or later. She was not mistaken. The Marquis used his remaining strength to get out of the hammock, fell on his knees in front of her and burst into the harsh weeping of a useless old man. Bernarda capitulated because of the fire of male tears sliding across her lap through the silk. Despite her hatred for Sierva María, she confessed her relief at knowing she was alive.

'I've always understood everything except death,' she said.

Once again she locked herself in her room with honey and cacao, and when she emerged two weeks later she was a walking corpse. The Marquis had been aware of travel preparations since early that morning and paid no attention to them. Before the sun grew hot, he saw Bernarda ride through the large courtyard gate on the back of a gentle mule, followed by another carrying the baggage. She had often left in this way, without mule drivers or slaves, without saying goodbye to anyone or giving reasons for anything. But the Marquis knew that this time she was leaving and would not return, because along with her usual trunk she was taking the two urns full of pure gold that she had kept buried for years under her bed.

Sprawled in his hammock, the Marquis again felt the terror that his slaves would attack him with knives and he forbade them to enter the house even during the day. And so when Cayetano Delaura came to see him by order of the Bishop, he had to push open the door and walk in uninvited, since no one responded to his loud knocking. The mastiffs were in a frenzy in their cages, but he pressed ahead. In the orchard, wearing his Saracen djellaba and Toledan cap, the Marquis was taking his siesta in the hammock, his entire body covered by orange blossoms. Delaura observed him without waking him, and it was as if he were seeing Sierva María grown old, and broken by solitude. The Marquis woke and did not recognize him at first because of the patch over his eye. Delaura raised his hand, his fingers extended in a sign of peace.

'God keep you, Señor Marquis,' he said. 'How are you?'

'Here,' said the Marquis. 'Rotting away.'

With a languid hand he brushed aside the cobwebs of his siesta and sat up in the hammock. Cayetano apologized for entering without being invited. The Marquis explained that no one bothered to answer the door because they had lost the habit of receiving visitors. Delaura spoke in a solemn tone. 'His Grace the Bishop, who is very preoccupied and suffering from asthma, has sent me as his representative.' Once the initial formalities were over, he sat beside the hammock and went straight to the matter that burned inside him.

'I wish to inform you that the spiritual health of your daughter has been entrusted to me,' he said.

The Marquis thanked him and wanted to know how she was.

'She is well,' said Delaura, 'but I want to help her be better.'

He explained the significance and methodology of exorcism. He spoke of the power given by Jesus to his disciples to expel unclean spirits from bodies and to heal sickness and disease. He recounted the Gospel parable of Legion and the 2,000 swine inhabited by demons. The fundamental task, however, was to establish whether Sierva María was in reality possessed. He did not believe so, but he required the assistance of the Marquis to dispel any doubt. First of all, he said, he wanted to learn what his daughter was like before she entered the convent.

'I do not know,' said the Marquis. 'I feel as if the more I know her the less I know her.'

He was tormented by guilt for having abandoned her to her fate in the courtyard of the slaves. To this he attributed her silences, which could last for months, her explosions of irrational violence, the astuteness with which she outwitted her mother when the girl put the same bell that had been hung around her wrist on the cats. The greatest obstacle to knowing her was her habit of lying for pleasure.

'Like the blacks,' said Delaura.

'The blacks lie to us but not to each other,' said the Marquis.

In her bedroom, Delaura could distinguish at a glance between the grandmother's profusion of possessions and the new objects that belonged to Sierva María: the lifelike dolls, the wind-up ballerinas, the music boxes. On the bed, just as the Marquis had packed it, lay the little valise he had brought to the convent. The theorbo, covered with dust, had been flung into a corner. The Marquis explained that it was an Italian instrument fallen into disuse and he exaggerated the girl's ability to play it. In his distraction he began to tune the lute, and then not only played it from memory but sang the song he had sung with Sierva María.

It was a revelatory moment. The music told Delaura what the Marquis had not been able to say about his daughter. And the father was so moved he could not finish the song. He sighed.

'You cannot imagine how well the hat suited her.'

Delaura was infected by his emotion.

'I can see you love her very much,' he said.

'You cannot imagine how much,' said the Marquis. 'I would give my soul to see her.'

Once again Delaura felt that the Holy Spirit did not omit the slightest detail.

'Nothing could be easier,' he said, 'if we can prove she is not possessed.'

'Speak to Abrenuncio,' said the Marquis. 'He has said from the beginning that Sierva is healthy, but only he can explain it.'

Delaura saw his dilemma. Abrenuncio could be providential, but talking to him might have undesirable implications. The Marquis seemed to read his mind.

'He is a great man,' the Marquis said.

Delaura shook his head in a meaningful gesture.

'I am familiar with the files of the Holy Office,' he said.

'No sacrifice would be too great to have her back,' insisted the Marquis. And since Delaura did not react in any way, he concluded: 'I beg you, for the love of God.'

Delaura, his heart breaking, said, 'I implore you not to make my suffering worse.'

The Marquis did not persist. He picked up the valise on the bed and asked Delaura to take it to his daughter.

'At least she will know that I am thinking of her,' he said.

Delaura fled without saying goodbye. He put the valise under his cape, then wrapped himself in the cloak as protection against the driving rain. It took some time for him to realize that his inner voice was reciting verses of the song the Marquis had played on the theorbo. Lashed by the rain, he began to sing aloud and repeated it from memory to the end. In the district of the artisans he turned to the left at the hermitage, still singing, and knocked at Abrenuncio's door.

After a long silence, he heard faltering steps and a voice only half awake.

'Who is it!'

'The law,' said Delaura.

It was all he could think of to avoid shouting his own name. Abrenuncio opened the door, believing that representatives of the government were really there, and did not recognize him. 'I am the librarian for the diocese,' said Delaura. The physician stepped aside to allow him through the dark entrance and helped him remove his soaked cape. In his characteristic fashion, Abrenuncio asked in Latin, 'In what battle did you lose that eye?'

Delaura recounted the mishap of the eclipse in classical Latin, telling him in detail about the persistence of the ailment despite the assurances of the Bishop's doctor that the patch was infallible. But Abrenuncio paid attention only to the purity of his language.

'It is absolute perfection,' he said in astonishment. 'Where are you from?'

'From Ávila,' said Delaura.

'Then it is even more praiseworthy,' said Abrenuncio.

He had him take off his cassock and sandals, and set them to dry, and placed his own libertine's cape over Delaura's muddied breeches. Then he removed the patch and tossed it in the trash bin. 'The only thing wrong with that eye is that it sees more than it ought to,' he said. Delaura was fascinated by the quantity of books crammed into the room. Abrenuncio observed this and led him to his dispensary, where there were many more volumes, on shelves that reached to the ceiling.

'By the Holy Spirit!' exclaimed Delaura. 'This is the library of Petrarch.'

'With some 200 books more than he had,' said Abrenuncio.

He allowed the visitor to browse at his pleasure. There were unique volumes that could have meant prison in Spain. Delaura recognized them, leafed through them with eagerness and replaced them on the shelves with regret in his soul. He found the eternal *Fray Gerundio* in a privileged position, along with a complete Voltaire in French and a translation into Latin of the *Lettres philosophiques*.

'Voltaire in Latin is almost a heresy,' he said as a joke.

Abrenuncio told him that it had been translated by a monk in Coimbra who permitted himself the luxury of making rare books for the solace of pilgrims. As Delaura looked through the volume, the physician asked whether he knew French.

'I do not speak it, but I read it,' said Delaura in Latin. And he added with no false modesty, 'As well as Greek, English, Italian, Portuguese and a little German.'

'I ask because of your remark about Voltaire,' said Abrenuncio. 'His is a perfect prose.'

'And the one that wounds us most,' said Delaura. 'What a shame it was written by a Frenchman.'

'You say that because you are a Spaniard,' said Abrenuncio.

'At my age, and with so much mixing of bloodlines, I am no longer certain where I come from,' said Delaura. 'Or who I am.'

'No one knows in these kingdoms,' said Abrenuncio. 'And I believe it will be centuries before they find out.'

Delaura spoke but did not interrupt his perusal of the library. Then, without warning, as had happened so often in the past, he thought of the book confiscated by the rector of the seminary when he was twelve, and of the only episode he could recall, which he had repeated throughout his life to anyone who might help him identify it.

'Do you remember the title?' asked Abrenuncio.

'I never knew it,' said Delaura. 'And I would give anything to find out how the story ends.'

Not saying a word, the physician placed before him a volume that he recognized as soon as he saw it. It was an old Sevillian edition of *The Four Books of Amadís of Gaul*. Delaura trembled as he inspected it, realizing he was on the verge of becoming unredeemable. At last he dared to say, 'Do you know that this is a forbidden book?'

'Like the best novels of our time,' said Abrenuncio. 'And to replace them they now print nothing but treatises for learned men. What would the poor of our day read if they did not read novels of chivalry in secret?'

'There are others,' Delaura said. 'One hundred copies of the first edition of *Don Quijote* were read here in the same year they were printed.'

'Not read,' said Abrenuncio. 'They passed through customs on their way to other kingdoms.'

Delaura did not pay attention to Abrenuncio because he had at last identified the precious edition of *Amadís of Gaul*.

'Nine years ago this book disappeared from the hidden section of our library, and we were never able to trace it,' he said.

'I can well imagine,' said Abrenuncio. 'But there are other reasons for considering this a historic edition: for more than a year it circulated from hand to hand among at least eleven people, and at least three of them died. I am certain they were victims of some unknown effluvium.'

'My duty is to denounce you to the Holy Office,' said Delaura.

Abrenuncio treated it as a joke: 'Have I let slip some heresy?'

'I say this because you have in your possession a forbidden book that is not your property and you have not informed the authorities.'

'This book and many others,' said Abrenuncio, indicating the crowded shelves with a wide circle of his finger. 'But if that were the reason, you would have come long ago, and I would not have opened the door.' He turned toward Delaura and concluded in good humor: 'On the other hand, I am glad you have come now and given me the pleasure of seeing you here.'

'The Marquis, concerned for the fate of his daughter, suggested it,' said Delaura.

Abrenuncio had Delaura sit on a chair facing him, and they both surrendered to the vice of conversation while an apocalyptic storm convulsed the sea. The physician gave an intelligent and erudite discourse on the history of rabies since the beginning of the human race, the devastation it had wrought with impunity, and the millenarian inability of medical science to stop it. He offered lamentable examples of how it had always been confused with demonic possession, as had certain forms of madness and other disturbances of the spirit. As for Sierva María, after so many weeks it did not seem probable that she would contract the disease. The only risk at present, Abrenuncio concluded, was that she, like so many others, would die of the cruelty of the exorcism.

Delaura thought this last sentence an exaggeration worthy of medieval medicine, but he did not dispute it, for it favored his theological indications that the girl was not possessed. He said that Sierva María's three African languages, so different from Spanish and Portuguese, did not in any way have the satanic implications attributed to them in the convent. There were numerous statements regarding her notable physical strength, but none to the effect that it was supernatural. And no act of levitation or prophesying the future had been proved against her – two phenomena, in fact, that also served as secondary proofs of sainthood. Although Delaura had sought the support of distinguished members of his own order and even of other communities, none had dared challenge the acta of the convent or contradict popular credulity. He was aware as well that no one would be convinced by his opinion or Abrenuncio's, much less both taken together.

'It would be you and I against everyone else,' he said.

'Which is why I was surprised that you came,' said Abrenuncio. 'I am no more than hunted prey in the game preserve of the Holy Office.'

'The truth is I am not really sure why I have come,' said Delaura. 'Unless that child has been imposed on me by the Holy Spirit to test the strength of my faith.'

Saying this was enough to free him from the knot of sighs that oppressed him. Abrenuncio looked into his eyes, into the depths of his soul, and realized he was on the verge of tears.

'Do not torture yourself in vain,' he said in a soothing

tone. 'Perhaps you have come only because you needed to talk about her.'

Delaura felt naked. He stood, looked for the way to the door, and did not rush out only because he was half dressed. Abrenuncio helped him on with his damp clothing and at the same time attempted to detain him in order to continue their conversation. 'I could talk to you without stopping until the next century,' he said. He tried to keep him with a flask of transparent eye wash to cure the persistence of the eclipse on his retina. He called him back from the door to find the valise he had left somewhere in the house. But Delaura seemed trapped in mortal sorrow. He thanked Abrenuncio for the afternoon, the medical assistance, the eye wash, but all he conceded was the promise to return another day when he had more time.

Delaura could not bear the urgency of his desire to see Sierva María. He was at the door and did not appear to notice that night had fallen. The sky had cleared but the sewers had flooded in the downpour, and Delaura took to the middle of the street in water up to his ankles. The gatekeeper at the convent tried to bar his way because it was almost curfew. He moved her aside.

'By order of His Grace the Bishop.'

Sierva María woke with a start and did not recognize him in the darkness. He did not know how to explain why he had come at so unusual an hour and he seized on the first pretext he could think of: 'Your father wants to see you.'

The girl recognized the valise, and her face burned with fury.

'But I don't want to see him,' she said.

Disconcerted, he asked the reason.

'Because I don't,' she said. 'I'd rather die.'

Delaura tried to unfasten the strap around her healthy ankle, thinking that would please her.

'Leave me alone,' she said. 'Don't touch me.'

He ignored her, and the girl loosed a sudden storm of spittle in his face. He persevered and offered the other cheek. Sierva María continued to spit at him. Again he turned his cheek, intoxicated by the gust of forbidden pleasure rising from his loins. He closed his eyes and prayed with all his soul while she continued to spit at him, her ferocity increasing with his pleasure, until she realized that her rage was useless. Then Delaura witnessed the fearful spectacle of one truly possessed. Sierva María's hair coiled with a life of its own, like the serpents of Medusa, and green spittle and a string of obscenities in idolatrous languages poured from her mouth. Delaura brandished his crucifix, put it up to her face, and shouted in terror, 'Get thee hence, infernal beast, whoever thou art.'

His shouts incited those of the girl, who was about to break the buckles on her straps. The frightened warder rushed in and tried to subdue her, but only Martina, with her celestial ways, succeeded. Delaura fled.

The Bishop was disturbed that he had not come to read at supper. Delaura realized he was floating on a personal cloud where nothing in this world or the next mattered except the horrific image of Sierva María debased by the devil. He took refuge in the library but could not read. He prayed with exacerbated faith, sang the song of the theorbo, wept tears of burning oil that seared him deep inside. He opened Sierva María's valise and placed the articles on the table one by one. He came to know them, smelled them with his body's avid desire, loved them, spoke to them in obscene hexameters until he could tolerate no more. Then he bared his torso, took the iron scourge, which he had never dared to touch, from the drawer of the work table and began to flagellate himself with an insatiable hatred that would give him no peace until he had extirpated the last vestige of Sierva María from his heart. The Bishop, who had been waiting for him, found him writhing on the floor in a mire of blood and tears.

'It is the demon, Father,' Delaura said. 'The most terrible one of all.'

Five

The Bishop called him to account in his office and listened without indulgence to his complete unadorned confession, conscious that he was presiding not over a sacrament but a judicial hearing. The only leniency he showed him was to keep the true nature of his sin a secret, yet with no public explanation he stripped him of his dignities and privileges and sent him to the Amor de Dios Hospital to nurse the lepers. Delaura begged for the consolation of saying five-o'clock Mass for them, and the Bishop granted his request. He kneeled with a sense of profound relief, and together they said an Our Father. The Bishop blessed him and helped him to his feet.

'May God have mercy on you,' he said. And erased him from his heart.

Even after Cayetano's punishment had begun, high dignitaries of the diocese interceded on his behalf, but the Bishop was intractable. He rejected the theory that exorcists become possessed by the very demons they wish to cast out. His final argument was that Delaura had not confined himself to facing the demons with the unappealable authority of Christ, but had committed the impertinence of discussing matters of faith with them. It was this, the Bishop said, that compromised his soul and brought him to the verge of heresy. More surprising, however, was that the Bishop had been so harsh with his confidant for a fault that deserved no more than a penance of green candles.

Martina had taken charge of Sierva María with exemplary devotion. She was distraught at the rejection of her request for a pardon, but the girl did not realize it until one afternoon of embroidery on the terrace, when she looked up and saw her bathed in tears. Martina did not attempt to hide her despair. 'I would rather be dead than go on dying in this prison.'

Her only hope, she said, was that Sierva María had dealings with demons. She wanted to know who they were, what they were like, how to negotiate with them. The girl named six, and Martina identified one as an African demon who had once troubled her parents' house. She was cheered by renewed optimism.

'I'd like to talk to him,' she said. And she specified the message: 'In exchange for my soul.'

Sierva María took delight in the deception. 'He can't speak,' she said. 'You just look into his face and know what he's saying.' With utmost seriousness she promised to inform her of his next visit so she could meet with him.

Cayetano, for his part, had submitted with humility to the vile conditions at the hospital. The lepers, in a state of legal death, slept on dirt floors in palm hovels. Many could do no more than crawl. General treatment was administered on Tuesdays, which were exhausting. Cayetano imposed on himself the purifying sacrifice of washing the most disabled bodies in the troughs at the stables. This is what he was doing on the first Tuesday of the penance, his priestly dignity reduced to the coarse tunic worn by nurses, when Abrenuncio appeared on the sorrel the Marquis had presented to him.

'How is that eye?' he asked.

Cayetano gave him no opportunity to speak of his misfortune or pity his condition. He thanked him for the eye wash that had, in effect, erased the image of the eclipse from his retina.

'You have nothing to thank me for,' said Abrenuncio. 'I gave you the best treatment we know for solar blindness: drops of rainwater.'

He invited him for a visit. Delaura explained that he could not leave the hospital without permission. Abrenuncio attributed no importance to this. 'If you know the ills of these kingdoms, you must know that laws are not obeyed for more than three days,' he said. He placed his library at Cayetano's disposal so that he could continue his studies during his punishment. He listened with interest but with no illusions.

'I leave you with this enigma,' Abrenuncio concluded as he spurred his horse. 'No god could have created a talent like yours to waste it scrubbing lepers.'

On the following Tuesday, he brought him a gift of the volume of the *Lettres philosophiques* in Latin. Cayetano leafed through it, smelled its pages, calculated its value. The more he appreciated it the less he understood Abrenuncio.

'I would like to know why you are so kind to me,' he said.

'Because we atheists cannot live without clerics,' said Abrenuncio. 'Our patients entrust their bodies to us, but not their souls, and like the devil, we try to win them away from God.'

'That does not go along with your beliefs,' said Cayetano.

'Not even I know what those are.'

'The Holy Office knows,' said Cayetano.

Contrary to expectations, the barbed remark delighted Abrenuncio. 'Come to the house and we can discuss it at our leisure,' he said. 'I sleep no more than two hours a night, and only for brief periods, so anytime is fine.' He spurred his horse and rode away.

Cayetano soon learned that the loss of great power is never partial. The same people who once had courted him because of his privileged position drew back as if he had leprosy. His friends in secular arts and letters moved aside to avoid a collision with the Holy Office. But it did not matter to him. He had no room in his heart for anything but Sierva María, and even so it was not large enough to hold her. He was convinced that no oceans or mountains, no laws of earth or heaven, no powers of hell could keep them apart.

One night, in a stroke of audacious inspiration, he escaped from the hospital to find some way into the convent. There were four entrances: the main gate with the turnstile, another gate of the same size, which faced the sea, and two small service doors. The first two were impassable. From the beach it was easy for Cayetano to identify Sierva María's window in the prison pavilion because it was the only one no longer sealed. From the street he examined every centimeter of the building, searching in vain for a tiny breach that would allow him a foothold.

He was about to give up, when he remembered the tunnel used to supply the convent during the *Cessatio a Divinis*. Tunnels under barracks or convents were typical of the period. No fewer than six were known in the city, and over the years more were discovered, all of them worthy of a romantic adventure novel. A leper who had been a gravedigger told Cayetano about the one he was looking for: an abandoned sewer that connected the convent to an adjacent plot of land where the cemetery of the first Clarissans had been located a century before. The opening was just under the prison pavilion and faced a high, rugged wall that seemed inaccessible. But Cayetano managed to climb it after many failed attempts, just as he believed he would accomplish everything through the power of prayer.

The pavilion was a still water in the small hours of the morning. Certain that the guard slept elsewhere, Cayetano's only concern was Martina Laborde, snoring behind a half-closed door. Until that moment the tension of the adventure had held him aloft, but when he found himself outside the cell, the padlock hanging open in the ring, his heart went mad. He pushed the door with his fingertips, stopped living as the hinges creaked and saw Sierva María asleep in the light of the Sanctuary Lamp. She opened her eyes, but it took her a moment to recognize him in the burlap tunic worn by those who nursed lepers. He showed her his bloodied fingernails.

'I climbed the wall,' he said in a whisper.

Sierva María's expression did not change.

'What for?' she asked.

'To see you,' he said.

Dazed by the trembling of his hands and the cracks in his voice, he did not know what else to say.

'Go away,' said Sierva María.

He shook his head several times for fear his voice would fail him. 'Go away,' she repeated. 'Or I'll scream.' By now he was so close he could feel her virgin breath.

'Even if they kill me I will not go,' he said. Then all at once he felt as if he had passed beyond his terror, and he added in a firm voice: 'And so if you are going to scream, you can start now.'

She bit her lip. Cayetano sat on the bed and gave her a detailed account of his punishment but did not tell her the reasons for it. She understood more than he was capable of saying. She looked at him without fear and asked why he did not have the patch over his eye.

'I don't need it anymore,' he said, encouraged. 'Now when I close my eyes I see hair like a river of gold.'

He left after two hours, happy because Sierva María agreed to his returning if he brought her favorite pastries from the arcades. He came so early the following night that the convent was still awake, and she had lit the lamp in order to finish some embroidery for Martina. On the third night, he brought wicks and oil to keep the lamp burning. On the fourth night, a Saturday, he spent several hours helping her kill the lice that were proliferating again in the cell. When her hair was clean and combed, he felt the icy sweat of temptation once more. He lay down next to Sierva María, his breathing harsh and uneven and found her limpid eyes a hand's breadth from his own. They both became confused. He, praying in fear, did not look away. She dared to speak.

'How old are you?'

'I turned thirty-six in March,' he said.

She scrutinized him.

'You're an old man,' she said with a touch of derision. She stared at the lines on his forehead and added with all the pitilessness of her years, 'A wrinkled old man.' He took it with good humor. Sierva María asked why he had a lock of white hair.

'It is a birthmark,' he said.

'Artificial,' she said.

'Natural,' he said. 'My mother had it too.'

He had not stopped looking into her eyes, and she showed no signs of faltering. He gave a deep sigh and recited, '*O sweet treasures, discovered to my sorrow*.'

She did not understand.

'It is a verse by the grandfather of my great-great-grandmother,' he explained. 'He wrote three eclogues, two elegies, five songs and forty sonnets. Most of them for a Portuguese lady of very ordinary charms who was never his, first because he was married, and then because she married another man and died before he did.'

'Was he a priest too?'

'A soldier,' he said.

Something stirred in the heart of Sierva María, for she wanted to hear the verse again. He repeated it, and this time he continued, in an intense, well-articulated voice, until he had recited the last of the forty sonnets by the cavalier of amours and arms Don Garcilaso de la Vega, killed in his prime by a stone hurled in battle.

When he had finished, Cayetano took Sierva María's hand and placed it over his heart. She felt the internal clamor of his suffering.

'I am always in this state,' he said.

And without giving his panic an opportunity, he unburdened himself of the dark truth that did not permit him to live. He confessed that every moment was filled with thoughts of her, that everything he ate and drank tasted of her, that she was his life, always and everywhere, as only God had the right and power to be, and that the supreme joy of his heart would be to die with her. He continued to speak without looking at her, with the same fluidity and passion as when he recited poetry, until it seemed to him that Sierva María was sleeping. But she was awake, her eyes, like those of a startled deer, fixed on him. She almost did not dare to ask.

'And now?'

'And now nothing,' he said. 'It is enough for me that you know.'

He could not go on. Weeping in silence, he slipped his arm beneath her head to serve as a pillow, and she curled up at his side. And so they remained, not sleeping, not talking, until the roosters began to crow and he had to hurry to arrive in time for five-o'clock Mass. Before he left, Sierva María gave him the beautiful necklace of Oddúa: eighteen inches of mother-of-pearl and coral beads.

Panic had been replaced by the yearning in his heart. Delaura knew no peace, he carried out his tasks in a haphazard way, he floated until the joyous hour when he escaped the hospital to see Sierva María. He would reach the cell gasping for breath, soaked by the perpetual rains, and she would wait for him with so much longing that only his smile allowed her to breathe again. One night she took the initiative with the verses she had learned after hearing them so often. '*When I stand and contemplate my fate and see the path along which you have led me*,' she recited. And asked with a certain slyness, 'What's the rest of it?'

'*I reach my end, for artless I surrendered to one who is my undoing and my end*,' he said.

She repeated the lines with the same tenderness, and so they continued until the end of the book, omitting verses, corrupting and twisting the sonnets to suit themselves, toying with them with the skill of masters. They fell asleep exhausted. At five the warder brought in breakfast, to the uproarious crowing of the roosters, and they awoke in alarm. Life stopped for them. The guard placed the food on the table, made a routine inspection with her lantern, and left without seeing Cayetano in the bed.

'Lucifer is quite a villain,' he mocked when he could breathe again. 'He has made me invisible too.'

Sierva María had to use all her cunning to keep the guard from coming back into the cell during the day. Late that night, after an entire day of play, they felt as if they had always been in love. Cayetano, half in jest and half in earnest, dared to loosen the laces of Sierva María's bodice. She protected her bosom with both hands, and a bolt of fury appeared in her eyes and a flash of red burned on her forehead. Cayetano grasped her hands with his thumb and index finger, as if they were in flames, and moved them away from her chest. She tried to resist, and he exerted a force that was tender but resolute.

'Say it with me,' he told her: '*Into your hands at last I have come vanquished*.'

She obeyed. '*Where I know that I must die*,' he continued, as he opened her bodice with icy fingers. And she repeated the lines almost in a whisper, trembling with fear: '*So that in myself alone it might be proven how deep the sword bites into conquered flesh*.' Then he kissed her on the mouth for the first time. Sierva María's body shivered in a lament, emitted a tenuous ocean breeze, and abandoned itself to its fate. He passed his fingertips over her skin almost without touching her, and experienced for the first time the miracle of feeling himself in another body. An inner voice told him how far he had been from the devil in his sleepless nights of Latin and Greek, his ecstasies of faith, the barren wastelands of his chastity, while she had lived with all the powers of untrammeled love in the hovels of the slaves. He allowed her to guide him, feeling his way in the darkness, but at the last moment he repented and in a moral cataclysm fell into the abyss. He lay on his back with his eyes closed. Sierva María was frightened by his silence, his stillness of death, and she touched him with her finger.

'What is it?' she asked.

'Let me be now,' he murmured. 'I am praying.'

In the days that followed they had no more than a few moments of calm while they were together. They never tired of talking about the sorrows of love. They exhausted themselves in kisses, they wept burning tears as they declaimed lovers' verses, they sang into each other's ear, they writhed in quicksands of desire to the very limits of their strength: spent, but virgin. For he had resolved to keep his vow until he received the sacrament, and she with him.

In the respites of passion they exchanged excessive proofs of their love. He said he would be capable of anything for her sake. With childish cruelty, Sierva María asked him to eat a cockroach. He caught one before she could stop him, and ate it live. In other senseless challenges he asked if she would cut off her braid for his sake, and she said yes but warned him, as a joke or in all seriousness, that if she did he would have to marry her to fulfill the terms of the promise. He brought a kitchen knife to the cell and said: 'We will see if it is true.' She turned so that he could cut it off at the root. She urged him on: 'I dare you.' He did not dare. Days later she asked if he would allow his throat to be slit like a goat's. He answered with a firm yes. She took out the knife and prepared to test him. He started in terror, feeling the final shudder. 'Not you,' he said. 'Not you.' She, overcome with laughter, wanted to know why, and he told her the truth, 'Because you really would do it.'

In the still waters of their passion they also began to experience the tedium of everyday love. She kept the cell clean and neat for the moment he arrived with all the naturalness of a husband returning home. Cayetano taught her to read and write and initiated her into the cults of poetry and devotion to the Holy Spirit, anticipating the happy day when they would be free and married.

At dawn on the twenty-seventh of April, Sierva María was just falling asleep after Cayetano had left the cell, when with no warning they came to begin the exorcism. It was the ritual of a prisoner condemned to death. They dragged her to the trough, wet her down with buckets of water, tore off her necklaces, and dressed her in the brutal shift worn by heretics. A gardener nun cut off her hair at the nape of the neck with four bites of her pruning shears and threw it into the fire burning in the courtyard. The barber nun clipped the ends to a half-inch, the length worn by Clarissans under the veil, and tossed them into the fire as she cut them. Sierva María saw the golden conflagration and heard the crackle of virgin wood and smelled the acrid odor of burned horn and did not move a muscle of her stony face. Then they put her in a straitjacket and draped her in funereal trappings, and two slaves carried her to the chapel on a military stretcher.

The Bishop had convoked the Ecclesiastical Council, composed of distinguished prebendaries, and they selected four of their number to assist him in the proceedings concerning Sierva María. In a final act of affirmation, the Bishop overcame his wretched ill health. He ordered the ceremony to be held not in the cathedral, as on other memorable occasions, but in the chapel of the Convent of Santa Clara, and he himself assumed responsibility for performing the exorcism.

The Clarissans, with the Abbess at their head, had been in the chancel since the small hours of the morning, and there they sang Matins to an organ accompaniment, moved by the solemnity of the day that was dawning. This was followed by the entrance of the prelates of the Ecclesiastical Council, the provosts of three orders and the principals of the Holy Office. Aside from these last-mentioned officials, no civil authority was or would be present.

The last to enter was the Bishop in his ceremonial vestments, borne on a platform by four slaves and surrounded by an aura of inconsolable affliction. He sat facing the high altar, next to the marble catafalque used for important funerals, in a swivel armchair that made it easier for him to move his body. At the stroke of six the two slaves carried in Sierva María, lying on the stretcher in the straitjacket and still muffled in purple cloth.

The heat became intolerable during the singing of the Mass. The bass notes of the organ rumbled in the coffered ceiling and left almost no openings for the bland voices of the Clarissans, invisible behind the lattices of the chancel. The two half-naked slaves who had brought in Sierva María's stretcher stood guard next to it. At the end of the Mass they uncovered her and left her lying like a dead princess on the marble catafalque. The Bishop's slaves moved his armchair next to her and left them alone in the large space in front of the high altar.

What followed produced unendurable tension and absolute silence, and seemed the prelude to some celestial prodigy. An acolyte placed the basin of holy water within reach of the Bishop. He seized the hyssop as if it were a battle hammer, leaned over Sierva María, and sprinkled the length of her body with holy water as he intoned a prayer. Then he uttered the conjuration that made the foundations of the chapel shudder.

'Whoever you may be,' he shouted, 'I command you in the name of Christ, Lord God of all that is visible and invisible, of all that is, was, and will be, to abandon this body redeemed by baptism, and return to darkness.'

Sierva María, beside herself with terror, shouted too. The Bishop raised his voice to silence her, but she shouted even louder. The Bishop took a deep breath and opened his mouth again to continue the exorcism, but the air died inside his chest and he could not expel it. He fell face forward, gasping like a fish on land, and the ceremony ended in an immense uproar.

That night Cayetano found Sierva María shivering with fever inside the straitjacket. What incensed him most was the mockery of her cropped head. 'God in Heaven,' he murmured with silent rage as he freed her from her bonds. 'How can you permit this crime?' As soon as she was free, Sierva María threw herself on his neck, and they embraced while she wept. He allowed her to give vent to her feelings. Then he raised her face and said, 'No more tears.' And coupled this with Garcilaso: '*Those I have wept for your sake are enough*.'

Sierva María recounted her terrible experience in the chapel. She told him about the deafening choirs that sounded like war, about the demented shouts of the Bishop, about his burning breath, about his beautiful green eyes ablaze with passion.

'He was like the devil,' she said.

Cayetano tried to calm her. He assured her that despite his titanic corpulence, his bellowing voice, his martial methods, the Bishop was a good and wise man. And so Sierva María's fear was understandable, but she was in no danger.

'What I want is to die,' she said.

'You feel enraged and defeated, and so do I because I cannot help you,' he said. 'But God will reward us on the day of resurrection.'

He took off the necklace of Oddúa that Sierva María had given him and put it around her neck to replace all the others. They lay down side by side on the bed and shared their rancor, while the world grew quiet until the only sound was the gnawing of termites in the coffered ceiling. Her fever subsided. Cayetano spoke in the darkness.

'The Apocalypse prophesies a day that will never dawn,' he said. 'Would to God it were today.'

Sierva María had been sleeping for about an hour after Cayetano left, when a new noise woke her. Standing before her, accompanied by the Abbess, was an old priest of imposing stature, with dark skin weathered by salt air, coarse bushy hair, heavy eyebrows, rough hands, and eyes that invited confidence. Sierva María was still half asleep when the priest said in Yoruban, 'I have brought your necklaces.'

He took them from his pocket, just as the superior of the convent had returned them to him in response to his demands. As he hung them around Sierva María's neck, he named and defined each one in African languages: the red and white of the love and blood of Changó, the red and black of the life and death of Elegguá, the seven aqua and pale blue beads of Yemayá. He moved with subtle tact from Yoruban to Congolese and from Congolese to Mandingo, and she followed suit with grace and fluency. If at the end he changed to Castilian, it was only out of consideration for the Abbess, who could not believe that Sierva María was capable of so much sweetness.

He was Father Tomás de Aquino de Narváez, a former prosecutor of the Holy Office in Seville and now parish priest in the slave district, whom the Bishop, his health impaired, had selected to replace him in the exorcism. His record of severity left no room for doubt. He had brought eleven heretics, Jews and Muslims, to the stake, but his reputation was based above all on the countless souls he had wrested away from the most cunning demons in Andalusia. He had refined tastes and manners and the sweet diction of the Canaries. He had been born here, the son of a royal solicitor who married his quadroon slave, and he had spent his novitiate in the local seminary once the purity of his lineage over four generations of whites had been demonstrated. His distinguished achievements earned him a doctorate at Seville, where he lived and preached until he was fifty. On his return to his native land, he requested the humblest parish, became an enthusiast of African religions and languages and lived among the slaves like a slave. No one seemed more capable of communicating with Sierva María and better prepared to confront her demons.

Sierva María recognized him at once as an archangel of salvation, and she was not mistaken. In her presence he took apart the arguments in the acta and proved to the Abbess that none of them was conclusive. He informed her that the demons of America were the same as those of Europe but that summoning them and controlling them were different. He explained the four common rules for recognizing demonic possession and helped her see how easy it was for the demon to manipulate these so that the opposite would be believed. He took his leave of Sierva María with an affectionate pinch of her cheek.

'Sleep well,' he said. 'I have dealt with worse enemies.'

The Abbess was so well disposed that she invited him to have a cup of the celebrated aromatic chocolate of the Clarissans, with the anisette biscuits and confectionary miracles reserved for the elect. As they ate and drank in her private refectory, he imparted his instructions for the measures that were to be taken next. The Abbess was happy to comply.

'I have no interest in whether or not things go well for that unhappy creature,' she said. 'What I do beg of God is that she leave this convent at once.'

The priest promised he would make every effort to have that be a matter of days, or hours, God willing.

Both were content when they said goodbye in the locutory, and neither could imagine they would never see each other again.

But that is what happened. Father Aquino, as his parishioners called him, set off on foot for his church, since for some time he had prayed very little and made amends to God by reviving the martyrdom of his nostalgia every day. He lingered at the arcades, overwhelmed by the hawking of peddlers who sold everything imaginable, and waited for the sun to go down before crossing the bog of the port. He bought the cheapest pastries and a partial ticket in the lottery of the poor, with the incorrigible hope of winning so that he could restore his dilapidated temple. He spent half an hour talking to the black matrons who sat on the ground like monumental idols beside handmade trinkets displayed on jute mats. At about five he crossed the Getsemaní drawbridge, where they had just hung the carcass of a large, sinister dog so that everyone would know it had died of rabies. The air carried the scent of roses, and the sky was the most diaphanous in the world.

The slave district, at the very edge of the salt marsh, was staggering in its misery. People lived alongside turkey buzzards and pigs in mud huts with roofs of palm, and children drank from the swamp in the streets. But with its intense colors and radiant voices it was the liveliest district, and even more so at twilight, when the residents carried chairs into the middle of the street to enjoy the cool air. The priest distributed the pastries among the children of the marsh, and kept three for his supper.

Thc temple was a mud-and-cane shack with a roof of

bitter palm and a wooden cross on its ridge. It had rough plank benches, a single altar with a single saint, and a wooden pulpit where Father Aquino preached on Sundays in African languages. The parish house was an extension of the church behind the altar, where the priest lived in austere conditions in one room that held a cot and a crude chair. In the rear were a small, rocky courtyard and an arbor with clusters of blighted grapes, and a fence of thornbushes that separated the courtyard from the marsh. The only drinking water was in a concrete cistern in one corner of the yard.

An old sacristan and an orphan girl of fourteen, both converted Mandingos, assisted him in the church and in the house, but were not needed after the Rosary. Before he closed the door, the priest ate the three pastries with a glass of water, and then, with his habitual formula in Castilian, he took his leave of the neighbors sitting in the street: 'May God grant all of you a blessed good night.'

At four in the morning, the sacristan, who lived a block away from the church, began to ring the bell for Mass. Before five o'clock, in view of the fact that the priest was late, the sacristan looked for him in his room. He was not there or in the courtyard. He continued looking in the vicinity of the church, for the priest sometimes visited nearby courtyards very early in the day to talk to the neighbors. He told the few parishioners who came to the church that there would be no Mass because the priest was nowhere to be found. At eight o'clock, with the sun already hot, the servant girl went to the cistern for water, and there was Father Aquino, floating on his back and wearing the breeches he kept on when he slept. It was a sad, widely mourned death, and a mystery that was never solved, which the Abbess proclaimed as definitive proof of demonic animosity toward her convent.

The news did not reach the cell of Sierva María, who waited for Father Aquino with innocent hopefulness. She could not explain to Cayetano who he was, but she did convey her gratitude for the return of the necklaces and his promise to rescue her. Until that moment it had seemed to both of them that love was enough to make them happy. In her disenchantment with Father Aquino, it was Sierva María who realized that their freedom depended only on themselves. Late one night, after long hours of kisses, she pleaded with Delaura not to go. He did not think she was serious, and said goodbye with one more kiss. She leaped from the bed and stretched her arms across the door.

'Either you stay or I'm going with you.'

She had once told Cayetano that she would like to take refuge with him in San Basilio de Palenque, a settlement of fugitive slaves twelve leagues from here, where she was sure to be received like a queen. It seemed a providential idea to Cayetano, but he did not connect it to their escape. He put his trust instead in legal formalities. In the Marquis's recovering his daughter with undeniable proof she was not possessed and in his obtaining the Bishop's pardon and permission to join a lay community where the marriage of a priest or nun would be so common it would shock no one. And so when Sierva María forced him to choose between staying and taking her with him, he tried once again to distract her. She clung to his neck and threatened to scream. Day was dawning. A frightened

Delaura managed to break away with a shove and fled just as they were beginning to sing Matins.

Sierva María's reaction was ferocious. She scratched the warder's face at the most trivial provocation, locked herself in with the crossbar and threatened to burn the cell and herself inside it if they did not let her go. The warder, in a rage because of her bloodied face, shouted, 'Just you dare, you beast of Beelzebub.'

Sierva María's only reply was to set fire to the mattress with the Sanctuary Lamp. The intervention of Martina and her soothing ways prevented a tragedy. In any event, in her daily report the warder requested that the girl be transferred to a more secure cell in the cloistered pavilion.

Sierva María's urgency heightened Cayetano's own longing to find an immediate solution other than flight. On two occasions he attempted to see the Marquis, and both times he was stopped by the mastiffs, out of their cages and roaming free in the house with no master. The truth was that the Marquis would never live there again. Conquered by his interminable fears, he had tried to seek refuge in the shelter of Dulce Olivia, but she did not open her door to him. Ever since the onset of his solitary grief, he had called on her by every means at his disposal and had received nothing but mocking responses on little paper birds. Then, without warning, she appeared, unsummoned and unannounced. She had swept and cleaned the kitchen, in a shambles through lack of use, and on the stove a pot bubbled over a cheerful flame. She was dressed for Sunday in organza flounces, and brightened by the latest cosmetics and ointments, and the only sign of her madness was a hat with an enormous brim trimmed in fabric fish and birds. 'I thank you for coming,' said the Marquis. 'I was feeling very lonely.' And he concluded with a lament, 'I have lost Sierva.'

'It's your fault,' she said in an offhand way. 'You did everything you could to lose her.'

Their supper was a stew in the local style, with three kinds of meat and the best of the vegetable garden. Dulce Olivia served it as if she were the mistress of the house, her manners well suited to her costume. The fierce dogs followed her everywhere, panting and winding themselves around her legs, and she beguiled them with the murmurings of a bride. She sat across the table from the Marquis, just as they might have been when they were young and not afraid of love, and they ate in silence without looking at each other, dripping with perspiration and eating their soup with an old married couple's lack of interest. After the first course Dulce Olivia paused to sigh and became aware of her age.

'This is how we could have been,' she said.

The Marquis found her bravado contagious. He looked at her: she was fat and old, two teeth were missing, and her eyes were withered. This is how they could have been, perhaps, if he had found the courage to oppose his father.

'When you are like this you seem to be in your right mind,' he said.

'I always have been,' she said. 'It was you who never saw me as I really was.'

'I picked you out of the crowd when you were all young and beautiful and it was difficult to choose the best,' he said.

'I picked myself out for you,' she said. 'Not you. You were always what you are now: a miserable devil.'

'You insult me in my own house,' he said.

The brewing argument excited Dulce Olivia. 'It's as much mine as yours,' she said. 'As the girl is mine, even though a bitch whelped her.' And not giving him time to reply, she concluded, 'And worst of all are the evil hands you've left her in.'

'She is in the hands of God,' he said.

Dulce Olivia shrieked in fury.

'She is in the hands of the Bishop's son, who has made her into his pregnant whore.'

'If you bit your tongue you would poison yourself,' shouted the Marquis, appalled.

'Sagunta exaggerates but she doesn't lie,' said Dulce Olivia. 'And don't try to humiliate me, because I'm the only one you have left to powder your face when you die.'

It was the invariable finale. Her tears began to fall into her plate like drops of soup. The dogs were asleep but the tension of the quarrel woke them, and they raised their watchful heads and growled deep in their throats. The Marquis felt as if he did not have enough air.

'You see,' he said in a fury, 'this is how we would have been.'

She stood without finishing her meal. She cleared the table, washed the dishes and casseroles with sordid fury, and as she washed each one she smashed it against the basin. He let her cry until she threw the pieces of crockery, like an avalanche of hail, into the trash bin. She left without saying goodbye. The Marquis never knew, and no one else ever knew, just when Dulce Olivia had stopped being herself and become no more than a nocturnal apparition in the house.

The fiction that Cayetano Delaura was the Bishop's son had replaced the older rumor that they had been lovers ever since Salamanca. Dulce Olivia's version, confirmed and distorted by Sagunta, said in effect that Sierva María, sequestered in the convent to satiate the satanic appetites of Cayetano Delaura, had conceived a child with two heads. Their saturnalias, Sagunta said, had contaminated the entire community of Clarissans.

The Marquis never recovered. Stumbling through the quagmire of the past, he searched for a refuge against his terror and found only the image of Bernarda, ennobled by his solitude. He tried to conjure it away by recalling the things he hated most about her: her fetid gases, her ill-tempered remarks, her bunions as sharp as a rooster's claws, and the more he tried to vilify her the more idealized his recollections became. Defeated by nostalgia, he sent exploratory messages to the sugar plantation at Mahates, where he supposed she had gone when she left the house, and she was there. He sent word that she should forget her anger and come home, so they might at least each have someone to die with. When he received no reply, he went to see her.

He had to find his way back along the streams of memory. The estate that had been the best in the viceregency was reduced to nothing. It was impossible to distinguish the road from the undergrowth. All that remained of the mill was rubble, machinery eaten away by rust, the skeletons of the last two oxen still yoked to the wheel. The pool of sighs in the shade of the calabash trees was the only thing that seemed alive. Before he could see the house through the burned brambles of the canebrakes, the Marquis smelled the scent of Bernarda's soaps, which had become her natural odor, and he realized how much he longed to be with her. And there she was, sitting in a rocking chair on the front veranda and eating cacao, her unmoving eyes fixed on the horizon. She wore a tunic of rose-colored cotton, and her hair was still damp from a recent bath in the pool of sighs.

The Marquis greeted her before climbing the three stairs to the gallery, 'Good afternoon.' Bernarda replied without looking at him, as if it were no one's greeting. The Marquis went up to the veranda, and from there he looked out over the brambles and searched the entire horizon in a single, uninterrupted glance. For as far as he could see, there was nothing but wild brush and the calabash trees at the pool. 'Where are all the people?' he asked. Bernarda, like her father, answered a second time without looking at him. 'They all left,' she said. 'There's not a living soul for a hundred leagues around.'

He went inside to find a chair. The house was in ruins, and plants with small purple flowers were breaking through the bricks of the floor. In the dining room he saw the old table, the same chairs devoured by termites, the clock that had been stopped at the same hour for longer than anyone could remember, all of it in an air filled with invisible dust that he could feel with each breath. The Marquis carried out one of the chairs, sat down next to Bernarda, and said in a very quiet voice, 'I have come for you.'

Bernarda's expression did not change, but she nodded her head in almost imperceptible affirmation. He described his life: the solitary house, the slaves crouching behind the hedges with their knives at the ready, the interminable nights.

'That is not living,' he said.

'It never was,' she said.

'Perhaps it could be,' he said.

'You wouldn't say that to me if you really knew how much I hate you,' she said.

'I have always thought I hated you too,' he said, 'and now it seems I am not so certain.'

Then Bernarda opened her heart so that he could see what was there in the light of day. She told him how her father had sent her to him, using the pretext of herrings and pickles, how they had deceived him with the old ruse of reading his palm, how they had decided she would violate him when he played the innocent, and how they had planned the cold, certain move of conceiving Sierva María and trapping him for life. The only thing he had to thank her for was that she did not have the heart to take the final step planned with her father, which was to pour laudanum in his soup so they would not have to suffer his presence.

'I put the noose around my own neck,' she said. 'But I'm not sorry. It was too much to expect that on top of everything else I'd have to love that poor premature creature, or you, when you've been the cause of my misfortunes.'

But the final step in her degradation had been the loss of Judas Iscariote. Searching for him in other men, she had given herself over to unrestrained fornication with the slaves on the plantation, something she had always thought repugnant before daring it for the first time. She chose them in crews and dispatched them one by one on the paths between the canebrakes until the fermented honey and the cacao tablets shattered her beauty, and she became swollen and ugly, and they did not have the courage to take on so much body. Then she began to pay. At first with trinkets for the younger ones, according to their looks and size, and in the end with pure gold for anyone she could find. By the time she discovered that they were fleeing in droves to San Basilio de Palenque to escape her insatiable craving, it was too late.

'Then I learned that I would have been capable of hacking them to pieces with a machete,' she said, not shedding a tear. 'And not only them but you and the girl, and my skinflint of a father, and everyone else who turned my life to shit. But I was no longer in any condition to kill anybody.'

They sat in silence, watching night fall over the brambles. A flock of distant animals could be heard on the horizon, and a woman's inconsolable voice calling them by name, one by one, until it was dark. The Marquis sighed.

'I see now that I have nothing to thank you for.'

He stood without haste, put the chair back in its place, and left the way he had come, not saying goodbye and not carrying a light. All that remained of him – a skeleton eaten away by turkey buzzards – was found two summers later on a path leading nowhere.

Martina Laborde had spent that entire morning embroidering in order to complete a piece that had taken longer than expected. She had her midday meal in Sierva María's cell, and then went to her own cell for a siesta. In the afternoon, as she was finishing the last stitches, she spoke to the girl with unusual sadness.

'If you ever leave this prison, or if I leave first, always remember me,' she said. 'It will be my only glory.'

Sierva María did not understand until the following day, when she was awakened by the warder shouting that Martina was not in her cell. They searched every corner of the convent and could not find a trace of her except for a note, written in her flowery hand, which Sierva María discovered under her pillow: *I will pray three times a day that the two of you will be very happy*.

She was still overwhelmed by surprise when the Abbess came in with the vicar and other reverend sisters of her infantry, and a squad of guards armed with muskets. She stretched out a choleric hand to strike Sierva María and shouted: 'You are an accomplice and you will be punished.'

The girl raised her free hand with a determination that stopped the Abbess in her tracks.

'I saw them leave,' she said.

The Abbess was stunned.

'She was not alone?'

'There were six of them,' said Sierva María.

It did not seem possible, and even less so that they could leave by the terrace, whose only point of egress was the fortified courtyard. 'They had bat's wings,' said Sierva María, flapping her arms. 'They spread them on the terrace, and then they carried her away, flying, flying, to the other side of the ocean.' The captain of the patrol crossed himself in fear and fell to his knees.

'Hail Mary Most Pure,' he said.

'Conceived without sin,' they all said in a chorus.

It was a perfect escape, planned by Martina in absolute secrecy and down to the smallest detail, ever since she had discovered that Cayetano was spending his nights in the convent. The only thing she did not foresee, or did not care about, was the need to close the sewer entrance from the inside to avoid arousing suspicion. Those who investigated the escape found the tunnel open, explored it, learned the truth, and sealed both ends without delay. Sierva María was forced to move to a locked cell in the pavilion of those interred in life. That night, beneath a splendid moon, Cayetano tore his hands trying to break through the seal on the tunnel.

Driven by a demented force, he ran to find the Marquis. He pushed open the main door without knocking and entered the deserted house, whose interior light was the same as the light in the street, for the brilliant moon made the whitewashed walls seem transparent. Clean and neat, the furnishings in place, flowers in the urns: everything was perfect in the abandoned house. The groan of the hinges aroused the mastiffs, but Dulce Olivia silenced them with a martial command. Cayetano saw her in the green shadows of the courtyard, beautiful, phosphorescent, wearing the tunic of a marquise, her hair adorned by fresh camellias with a frenzied scent, and he raised his hand to form a cross with his index finger and thumb.

'In the name of God: Who are you?' he asked.

'A soul in torment,' she said. 'And you?'

'I am Cayetano Delaura,' he said, 'and I have come on bended knee to beg the Señor Marquis to listen to me for a moment.'

Dulce Olivia's eyes flashed in anger.

'The Señor Marquis is not interested in listening to a scoundrel,' she said.

'And who are you to speak with so much command?'

'I am the queen of this house,' she said.

'For the love of God,' said Delaura. 'Tell the Marquis that I have come to talk to him about his daughter.' And with his hand on his heart, he came to the point and said, 'I am dying of love for her.'

'One more word and I will turn loose the dogs,' said Dulce Olivia in indignation, and she pointed to the door, 'Get out of here.'

The power of her authority was so great that Cayetano backed out of the house in order not to lose sight of her.

On Tuesday, when Abrenuncio entered his cubicle at the hospital, he found Delaura devastated by mortal vigils. He told the doctor about everything, from the real reasons for his punishment to his nights of love in the cell. Abrenuncio was perplexed.

'I would have imagined anything about you except these extremes of lunacy.'

Cayetano, bewildered in turn, asked, 'Have you never gone through this?'

'Never, my son,' said Abrenuncio. 'Sex is a talent, and I do not have it.'

Abrenuncio tried to dissuade him. He said that love was an emotion *contra natura* that condemned two strangers to a base and unhealthy dependence, and the more intense it was, the more ephemeral. But Cayetano did not hear him. He was obsessed with fleeing as far as possible from the oppression of the Christian world.

'Only the Marquis can help us with regard to the law,' he said. 'I wanted to get down on my knees and plead with him, but I did not find him at home.'

'You never will,' said Abrenuncio. 'He heard rumors that you attempted to abuse the girl. And now I see that from a Christian's point of view, he was not mistaken.' He looked into Cayetano's eyes. 'Aren't you afraid you will be damned?'

'I believe I already am, but not by the Holy Spirit,' said Delaura without alarm. 'I have always believed He attributes more importance to love than to faith.'

Abrenuncio could not hide the wonder caused in him by this man so recently freed from the shackles of reason. But he made no false promises, above all when the Holy Office loomed.

'You people have a religion of death that fills you with the joy and courage to confront it,' he said. 'I do not: I believe the only essential thing is to be alive.'

Cayetano raced to the convent. In the light of day he walked through the service door and crossed the garden, taking no precautions, convinced he had been made invisible through the power of prayer. He climbed to the second floor, walked down a solitary corridor with low ceilings that connected the two sections of the convent, and entered the silent, rarefied world of those interred in life. Without realizing it, he had walked past the new cell where Sierva María wept for him. He had almost reached the prison pavilion when a shout at his back stopped him.

'Halt!'

He turned and saw a nun with a veil covering her face and a crucifix held high against him. He took a step toward her, but the nun placed Christ between them. '*Vade retro*!' she shouted.

He heard another voice behind him: '*Vade retro*.' And then another, and another: '*Vade retro*.' He turned around several times and realized he was in the middle of a circle of phantasmagoric nuns with veiled faces who brandished their crucifixes and pursued him with their cries:

'*Vade retro, Satana*!'

Cayetano had reached the end of his strength. He was handed over to the Holy Office and condemned at a public trial that cast suspicions of heresy over him and provoked disturbances among the populace and controversies in the bosom of the Church. Through a special act of grace, he served his sentence as a nurse at the Amor de Dios Hospital, where he lived many years with his patients, eating and sleeping with them on the ground, and washing in their troughs with water they had used, but never achieving his confessed desire to contract leprosy.

Sierva María waited for him in vain. After three days she stopped eating, in an explosion of rebelliousness that exacerbated the signs of her possession. Shattered by the downfall of Cayetano, by the indecipherable death of Father Aquino, by the public resonance of a misfortune that went beyond his wisdom and his power, the Bishop resumed the exorcism with an energy that was inconceivable, given his condition and his age. This time Sierva María, confined in a straitjacket, her skull shaved by a razor, confronted him with satanic ferocity, speaking in tongues or with the shrieks of infernal birds. On the second day the immense bellowing of maddened cattle could be heard, the earth trembled and it was no longer possible to think that Sierva María was not at the mercy of all the demons of hell. When she returned to her cell, she was given an enema of holy water, which was the French method for expelling any devils that might remain in her belly.

The struggle continued for three more days. Although she had not eaten for a week, Sierva María managed to extricate one leg and kick her heel into the Bishop's lower abdomen, knocking him to the ground. Only then did they realize she had been able to free herself because her body was so emaciated that the straps no longer confined her. The ensuing outrage made it advisable to interrupt the exorcism – an action favored by the Ecclesiastical Council but opposed by the Bishop.

Sierva María never knew what happened to Cayetano Delaura, why he never came back with his basket of delicacies from the arcades and his insatiable nights. On the twenty-ninth of May, having lost her will to endure any more, she dreamed again of the window looking out on a snow-covered field from which Cayetano Delaura was absent and to which he would never return. In her lap she held a cluster of golden grapes that grew back as soon as she ate them. But this time she pulled them off not one by one but two by two, hardly breathing in her longing to strip the cluster of its last grape. The warder who came in to prepare her for the sixth session of exorcism found her dead of love in her bed, her eyes radiant and her skin like that of a newborn baby. Strands of hair gushed like bubbles as they grew back on her shaved head.

read more

Gabriel García Márquez

MEMORIES OF MY MELANCHOLY WHORES

'A Velvety pleasure to read. Márquez has composed, with his usual sensual gravity and Olympian humour, a love letter to the dying light.' John Updike

'The year I turned ninety, I wanted to give myself a gift of a night of wild love with an adolescent virgin…'

He has never married, never loved and never gone to bed with a woman he didn't pay. But on finding a young girl naked and asleep on the brothel owner's bed, a passion is ignited in his heart – and he feels, for the first time, the urgent pangs of love.

Each night, exhausted by her factory work, 'Delgadina' sleeps peacefully whilst he watches her quietly. During these solitary early hours, his love for her deepens and he finds himself reflecting on his newly found passion and the loveless life he has led. By day, his columns in the local newspaper are read avidly by those who recognise in his outpourings the enlivening and transformative power of love.

'Márquez describes this amorous, sometimes disturbing journey with the grace and vigour of a master storyteller' *Daily Mail*

'There is not one stale sentence, redundant word or unfinished thought' *The Times*

read more

Gabriel García Márquez

ONE HUNDRED YEARS OF SOLITUDE

'The greatest novel in any language of the last 50 years. Marquez writes in this lyrical, magical language that no-one else can do' Salman Rushdie

'Many years later, as he faced the firing squad, Colonel Aureliano Buendía was to remember that distant afternoon when his father took him to discover ice ...'

Pipes and kettledrums herald the arrival of gypsies on their annual visit to Macondo, the newly founded village where José Arcadio Buendía and his strong-willed wife, Úrsula, have started their new life. As the mysterious Melquíades excites Aureliano Buendía's father with new inventions and tales of adventure, neither can know the significance of the indecipherable manuscript that the old gypsy passes into their hands.

Through plagues of insomnia, civil war, hauntings and vendettas, the many tribulations of the Buendía household push memories of the manuscript aside. Few remember its existence and only one will discover the hidden message that it holds...

'Should be required reading for the entire human race' *New York Times*

'No lover of fiction can fail to respond to the grace of Márquez's writing' *Sunday Telegraph*

'It's the most magical book I have ever read. I think Márquez has influenced the world' Carolina Herrera

Gabriel García Márquez

IN EVIL HOUR

'A masterly book' *Guardian*

'César Montero was dreaming about elephants. He'd seen them at the movies on Sunday ...'

Only moments later, César is led away by police as they clear the crowds away from the man he has just killed.

But César is not the only man to be riled by the rumours being spread in his Colombian hometown – under the cover of darkness, someone creeps through the streets sticking malicious posters to walls and doors. Each night the respectable townsfolk retire to their beds fearful that they will be the subject of the following morning's lampoons.

As paranoia seeps through the town and the delicate veil of tranquility begins to slip, can the perpetrator be uncovered before accusation and violence leave the inhabitants' sanity in tatters?

'*In Evil Hour* was the book which was to inspire my own career as a novelist. I owe my writing voice to that one book!' Jim Crace

'Belongs to the very best of Márquez's work … Should on no account be missed' *Financial Times*

'A splendid achievement' *The Times*

GABRIEL GARCÍA MÁRQUEZ

CHRONICLE OF A DEATH FORETOLD

'My favourite book by one of the world's greatest authors. You're in the hands of a master' Mariella Frostrup

'On the day they were going to kill him, Santiago Nasar got up at five-thirty in the morning to wait for the boat the bishop was coming on …'

When newly-wed Angela Vicario and Bayardo San Román are left to their wedding night, Bayardo discovers that his new wife is no virgin. Disgusted, he returns Angela to her family home that very night, where her humiliated mother beats her savagely and her two brothers demand to know her violator, whom she names as Santiago Nasar.

As he wakes to thoughts of the previous night's revelry, Santiago is unaware of the slurs that have been cast against him. But with Angela's brothers set on avenging their family honour, soon the whole town knows who they plan to kill, where, when and why.

'A masterpiece' *Evening Standard*

'A work of high explosiveness – the proper stuff of Nobel prizes. An exceptional novel' *The Times*

'Brilliant writer, brilliant book' *Guardian*

read more

GABRIEL GARCÍA MÁRQUEZ

LOVE IN THE TIME OF CHOLERA

'An amazing celebration of the many kinds of love between men and women'
The Times

'It was inevitable: the scent of bitter almonds always reminded him of the fate of unrequited love …'

Fifty-one years, nine months and four days have passed since Fermina Daza rebuffed hopeless romantic Florentino Ariza's impassioned advances and married Dr. Juvenal Urbino instead. During that half century, Florentino has fallen into the arms of many delighted women, but has loved none but Fermina. Having sworn his eternal love to her, he lives for the day when he can court her again.

When Fermina's husband is killed trying to retrieve his pet parrot from a mango tree, Florentino seizes his chance to declare his enduring love. But can young love find new life in the twilight of their lives?

'A love story of astonishing power and delicious comedy' *Newsweek*

'A delight' Melvyn Bragg

read more

GABRIEL GARCÍA MÁRQUEZ

THE STORY OF A SHIPWRECKED SAILOR

'A gripping tale of survival' *The Times*

'On February 22 we were told that we would be returning to Columbia …'

In 1955, eight crew members of *Caldas*, a Colombian destroyer, were swept overboard. Velasco alone survived, drifting on a raft for ten days without food or water. Márquez retells the survivor's amazing tale of endurance, from his loneliness and thirst to his determination to survive.

The Story of a Shipwrecked Sailor was Márquez's first major, and controversial, work, published in a Colombian newspaper, *El Espectador*, in 1955 and then in book form in 1970.

'The story of Velasco on his raft, his battle with sharks over a succulent fish, his hallucinations, his capture of a seagull which he was unable to eat, his subsequent droll rescue, has all the grip of archetypal myth. Reads like an epic' *Independent*